SCAR-STRUCK
A ROMANTIC COMEDY

Scar-Struck
Copyright © 2025

First Published February 2025

The moral rights of the author have been asserted.
All rights reserved.

This book may not be reproduced in whole or in part, stored, posted on the internet, or transmitted in any form or by any means, whether electronically, mechanically, or by photocopying, recording, sharing or any other means, without written permission from the author and publisher of the book. All content found online or offline without written permission will be breaking the copyright law and, therefore, render you liable and at risk of litigation.

Cover: Stargazer Creative Studio
www.stargazercreativestudio.com
Editing: Pagetrim Book Edit & Design Services
Formatting: Pagetrim Book Edit & Design Services
www.pagetrimservices.com

Published by Prana Publishing House

ISBN: 978-1-7638852-0-2

TABLE OF CONTENTS

Chapter 1 7
Chapter 2 12
Chapter 3 18
Chapter 4 30
Chapter 5 41
Chapter 6 51
Chapter 7 59
Chapter 8 70
Chapter 9 85
Chapter 10 107
Chapter 11 122
Chapter 12 130
Chapter 13 144
Chapter 14 153

SCAR-STRUCK
A ROMANTIC COMEDY

Mya Stevens

CHAPTER 1

"Hey, Char, phone for you—some bloke with a weird accent."

Charlotte looked up from pouring the first early-morning pint of the day. "Oh, okay, thanks Mave." She finished the 'breakfast beer' transaction with one of their regulars, wiped her hands on her bar apron and walked behind the gleaming wall of alcoholic beverages to pick up the old-fashioned receiver. She greeted the caller and heard an echo on the line.

"Hello, Miss Grant? My name is Marvin Kennedy, I'm from the office of Amanda Voss and am calling to inform you your application for a working visa has been approved. Congratulations, Miss Grant, you're coming to America!"

Charlotte's pulse quickened as her hand shot up to her agape mouth. *Shit! I must have got the job!*

"Miss Grant?" Kennedy asked after a short delay.

"Yes! Sorry, I'm here. Just can't believe it!" The phone line crackled and Charlotte heard her voice repeat a few seconds later.

"I understand your excitement, Miss Grant, it's an amazing opportunity. Not all Australian applicants land a job in the United States, let alone Hollywood! We have conducted the necessary checks with your training academy, so you'll shortly be receiving the contract for signing. We'll be sending it to the post office in—let me try to pronounce this word—Goon-der-gay?"

Charlotte stifled a snort. "We prefer "Fun-dah-guy, matey!"

"... Excuse me?"

Charlotte bit her lip. This wasn't the time to joke around. "Sorry, Mr Kennedy, it's pronounced Gun-dah-gai. You were close though!"

After an awkward silence, they confirmed some details and exchanged a few more pleasantries. Charlotte replaced the receiver on the bulky wooden handset attached to the wall. She gazed blankly at the numerous scratches, stains, numbers and rude drawings etched into the surface as her mind raced. *Oh my God... I'm going to Hollywood...*

She slowly wandered back behind the bar, picked up a glass and reached for a bottle of whisky, staring at nothing in particular. Barely registering what she was doing, she poured a measured shot into the glass, downed it in one and wiped her mouth with the back of her hand.

"You 'right, love? Bad news on the blower? Look like you seen a ghost!"

Charlotte snapped out of her daze and looked over at the three regulars lined up at the bar, the oldest of who was looking straight at her rather than the dusty old TV screen above her head. She smiled at him.

"Nah, all good, Merv. Thanks, mate." She paused, then smiled. "Really good news actually."

Merv nodded upwards, gave her a little wink and continued with his morning drink.

Her mind raced as she looked out through the patchy fly-screen door to the dusty brown hills in the distance. The morning sun hit the top of the colonial buildings lining the main road of their little country town. A hand suddenly touched her shoulder. She jumped.

"Shit, Char, you're a jumpy little thing!" said Mave. You okay? Geez you're pale! Who was that geezer on the phone?"

Without thinking, Charlotte pulled her boss into a hug, squeezing her tightly.

Mave responded with a motherly purr and patted her back gently. She released Charlotte and held her at arm's length, her eyebrows raised expectantly on her round, kind face.

Charlotte took a deep breath as Mave let her go and leaned one hand on the bar, waiting for her to tell all. You didn't keep secrets in Gundagai, particularly from Mave.

"So, you remember how I was travelling to Sydney every weekend for a while there? And had to take two weeks off during February... that really hard slog before I had exams?"

Mave's eyes narrowed, then her face lit up. "Oh yeah, you were doing a beauty course, weren't you? No, the make-up course!"

Charlotte nodded. "Yep, that's the one. Well, I finished the course, and I passed and was starting to look for casual work locally. But like, a few days after I was done, one of my instructors sent me an email. Said he really liked my work—not the glamour stuff, the 'formal normal' as I called it—I reckon I was a bit shit at that side of it... but the wounds, injuries—the makeup paired with the prosthesis sculpting, monsters, horror and that sort of thing? I guess I just took to it like a duck to water."

Mave smiled and rolled her eyes. "Trust you to be better at the blood and gore, never been a girly-girl have ya! And watching all those awful horror movies like you do... anyway yes, go on," she prompted with a wave.

"I was a bit suss because I didn't know about this instructor, and he seemed like a bit of a dickhead. Apparently, he was alright though... made some calls on my behalf. Turns out one of his mates needs people for a movie series they're about to start filming in America. He goes and gets me an interview with some mob—get this—in *Hollywood*!" Charlotte heard a few gasps around the bar, including one from her boss.

"Hells bells! Are you kidding me, darl? You kept all this bloody quiet, didn't you!" Mave's free hand flew to her chest.

Charlotte glanced over Mave's shoulder and scanned behind her—as suspected, every eye in the pub was looking straight at them, listening intently to her story.

"So, anyway, I did a Zoom interview last time I was in Sydney, couple weeks back. They asked me loads of questions and said they had seen pictures and videos of my work. I reckoned I'd stuffed it— was so nervous, shaking and saying stupid shit—you know me. But blow me if I didn't get the job! They arranged my working visa and everything, said they hadn't seen talent like mine in a long time!" She excitedly pointed in the direction of the phone using her thumb. "That was a guy from the make-up company, telling me they've already approved my working visa, and that I've got the job in Hollywood!"

The few patrons in the bar erupted with applause, and Charlotte heard, "Congrats darl!" and "Our Char, off to Hollywood!" and "you've made us proud" over the din.

Mave had tears as she pulled Charlotte in for another embrace.

"So bloody proud of you," she said warmly as the clapping and cheering died down. "Wait till I tell Kev; he's going to shit himself" Mave said, wiping the tears from her eyes. "How the hell am I going to find another you…?"

CHAPTER 2

"Right, I guess that's me then," Charlotte said, instinctively patting her jacket pockets, although she realised she no longer possessed keys to anything. They, along with the rest of her belongings, had been safely stored at the pub. Her father and brother still had keys to their family home, such as it was, however, Charlotte didn't want to take any chances. What remained in the house would likely be sold by her father for drinking money, so she ensured anything left there had no emotional attachment.

Mave, Kev, a few close friends and some locals walked along Sheridan Street to the bus stop to see Charlotte off. The coach to Sydney was scheduled to leave around 1:00 pm. Her suitcase wheels rolled over the footpath paving with a faint growl, barely audible over the loud chatter. When the crowd arrived at the bus stop, a few other people she knew vaguely were waiting. Charlotte looked across to Carberry Park in the early afternoon sunshine and saw two women laughing as they pushed kids on the swings. The surrounding hills looked a little greener now thanks to some much-needed rain in the past few weeks. Merv, her favourite pub regular, had demonstrated how significant Charlotte's departure was by leaving his bar seat, beer in hand, and accompanying them to the bus stop. A gentle wind carrying the smell of grass rustled the tall gum trees and caressed her face.

It suddenly hit her just how much she would miss home. A lump formed in her throat.

"Here, Char, I made you a little picnic hamper for the bus," said Kev, handing Charlotte a stuffed paper bag. "There's a big fat sanger in there for ya along with a few of your other faves. God knows what you'll have to eat in America. I want to get as much good Aussie food in your piehole while we can."

Charlotte looked at the bag, then at Kev's smiling face.

"Chippies in there, too, obviously," he said, and winked.

Tears erupted from Charlotte's eyes, and she launched herself at him, reaching her slender arms around his wide chest.

"Oh now, girly, it's okay, it's all okay! You're going to have an amazing adventure... you'll see a bunch of American weirdos, check out what those Hollywood phonies have to offer... then you'll get that skinny little arse of yours on a plane home to us, alright? Don't make Mave come over there and drag you back, because you know she will... would fly over with you given the chance, wouldn't you, darl?"

Charlotte heard his soothing voice muffled as she buried her face into his soft flannelette shirt. She felt the warmth of his words and another set of arms around her back and knew Mave was there, too. After some time, she extracted herself, stood back and wiped her wet face. "Sorry matey, your shirt is all covered in snot now."

"Ahh, not to worry, it's been covered in worse," Kev said dismissively.

Mave took Charlotte's arm and pulled her into another hug. Not known for displaying emotions in public, Charlotte felt Mave sobbing as she gently squeezed. Standing back, the two women wiped their faces and laughed.

"I look like a bloody panda now," Mave chuckled as she reached into her pocket for a tissue, giving one to Charlotte also. Kev put his arm around his wife and pulled her into his ribs.

"I'm sure your dad would be here if he could, and your little bro said he'd phone you in a couple of days once he's in a spot with reception. Just hard to get back from the construction site just now."

Charlotte nodded as she blew her nose. They were being kind, as always. *There's no way my dad would be here unless the drink ran out or he needed money... and I wouldn't want Dylan to jeopardise his new job for me. Everything's as it should be.*

Charlotte walked over to the garbage bin to deposit her now soaked tissue. As she looked up, she saw a familiar face ambling towards her. Charlotte beamed, recognising William, an elder of the native Wiradjuri people, approaching with a big smile and a slight limp. As she rushed towards him, she tripped on an uneven patch of footpath and stumbled. Helpful as ever, William stretched out his hands to catch her in an awkward embrace.

"Oh, William, I'm so glad to see you... I can't even make it to the bloody bin without tripping over my own feet, how am I going to survive halfway around the world?"

The elder laughed.

"Your head is heavy, girly... lots of thoughts," he said with a sly grin. "They weigh you down... means your feet don't work so good."

Charlotte laughed and squeezed his hands tighter.

"I'm so homesick already... I don't know if I can do this, William," she admitted, looking into his kind eyes, feeling hers welling up again and her bottom lip quivering. Charlotte always had the feeling the elder could see right through her—there was no point in hiding anything because he'd know the truth.

"Keep your energy in your feet, girly. They know the way home. They will know *bunji* and they will know liars. I've been to Hollywood, when I was your age. It's important to remember who you are."

Charlotte nodded and narrowed her eyes in thought as she listened, feeling like he had more to say.

"Whenever you feel lost, close your eyes. Feel the wind on your face, your feet on the ground. Hear the pulse of the earth. You can hear home, you can hear us. Hear your tribe. You'll remember who you are."

Tears flowed freely again down Charlotte's cheeks, and she nodded with understanding and gratitude. The elder let go of her hands and drew her into a warm embrace, patting her gently on the back.

"You'll be okay, Charlotte. You're ready for this next chapter... I'll let you get along now—looks like there are others waiting to say goodbye. I'll see you soon, girly." He winked as he patted her on the arm and started up the gentle incline of the main street.

Charlotte thanked him as he departed and wiped her face with her sleeve. She felt like she'd need to remember those wise words before too long.

As she strolled back to the bus stop, well-wishers took turns saying goodbye and uttering parting words. Although Charlotte didn't have many close friends, she could feel the love and support from her community, and it warmed her heart. The crowd was growing by the minute, with random passersby stopping to see what all the fuss was about. The mix of gratitude, surprise and impending fear swirled in her stomach uncomfortably, and secretly she wished the bus would just hurry up so she could ugly-cry in peace.

The bus trip from Gundagai to Sydney passed quickly. Charlotte had spent the first two hours weeping intermittently, but thankfully the bus was fairly empty, so she'd had some privacy to pour out her emotions. When the tears had seemingly dried up, and realising how hungry she suddenly was, she tucked into the bag of food Kev had lovingly prepared for her and read the little note inside:

We're so proud of our Char—go knock 'em dead, kiddo! xxx

Inside the picnic bag were thick ham and mustard sandwiches with the crusts cut off, little homemade pastries and pies, a fresh fruit salad with mint leaves and a few packets of her favourite potato chips. Shortly after eating the majority of the food, she'd fallen into a deep sleep and had awoken about an hour outside Sydney.

Later that evening, Charlotte sat on one of the mismatched wooden chairs on either side of the small, rickety table in her room in a Sydney hostel, and looked outside at the bustling streets below. A symphony of car horns, people yelling and laughing, the iconic sound of an Australian pedestrian crossing, the booming rhythm of the nearby train line which shook her tiny room every few minutes and the intense humidity came through her open window. Instead of the smell of grass and gum trees, a hot, pungent mix of exhaust fumes, cigarette smoke and hot asphalt met her nostrils and clung to her throat.

A party was taking place in the dormitory below her. A blood-curdling scream through the squeaky floorboards snapped her out of her stupor, and she leaned out of the window in curiosity. The scream was followed by raucous laughter, indicating all was well. People were yelling at each other down on the street and she could hear the loud clatter of metal garbage bins hitting the ground. *Is this what living in the city is really like? They're all nut bars!*

Charlotte glanced at her phone; it was very late, and tomorrow was a big day. She'd only have a few hours' sleep before catching the train to the airport, then her flight to L.A. She closed the window with its flimsy and inefficient catch, crawled into bed and clutched her scratchy, over-starched sheets tight to her chest. The surrounding noise continued to pound her senses until she eventually fell into a fitful sleep punctured by scenes from home and fear of the unknown.

CHAPTER 3

Charlotte's phone alarm went off at six, but she was already awake. The combination of jet lag, excitement and the squirmy nervous monster who'd taken up residence in her stomach had resulted in a restless night's sleep. She turned off the alarm and sat up. *Here we go...*

She made herself an espresso from the basic pod machine in her kitchenette and waited until the toast popped up. After stopping at the local grocery store down the road from her Hollywood apartment over the weekend, Charlotte had purchased a bag of the healthiest ingredients she could find to do a small batch cook of veggies and various other healthy snacks for the week, wanting to avoid any high fat and sugar products. Being uncertain about the day's working conditions, she figured that at least she'd have some good food to heat up when she returned home. Whenever that was.

The tiny studio rental apartment she'd secured through the agency was in need of minor repairs and a thorough clean, but

Charlotte didn't mind. She could easily attend to these things once settled, and much preferred her privacy over living with strangers. It was quiet, despite the busy streets outside, and her neighbours had so far kept to themselves. At least in response to Charlotte's enthusiastic greetings, which seemed to terrify most locals. As she leaned against the counter and ate her breakfast, Charlotte thought back to her recent flight.

The first leg to Honolulu—or 'Hono-one-loo' as Charlotte had dubbed it, since every ladies' toilets in the airport had plumbing maintenance issues—had been tolerable considering it was the first ever international trip she'd taken. Turbulence in a huge airbus was a novelty and Charlotte felt exhilarated by the sensation of bumping up and down as opposed to the fear response she saw in other passengers. After pressing every button repeatedly on the small console on the chair in front of her, she finally decided on a new release movie. Living in the countryside meant any new movie was a huge privilege. They didn't have a movie theatre in Gundagai, and she was never home to warrant paying for a streaming service subscription.

A gasp from the aisle seat to her right made Charlotte look; the passenger was holding the end of the arm rests, white knuckles popping, eyes shut tight, head back in his seat. *Poor bloke, he looks terrified...*

"Hey mate, you okay? Not a fan of the bumps, eh?" Charlotte asked quietly, gently patting the man's hand closest to hers. He flinched and opened his eyes wide, little beads of sweat popping out of his pale temples. Continuing to look up at the ceiling as if his life depended on it, he answered in a strangled American accent.

"No... I'm not okay... I'm petrified.... Why did I agree to cut short my holiday and go back for my goddamned ex-wife's wedding... I hate that woman. I hate flying... why the hell am I here?"

Grimacing, Charlotte tried to think of some comforting words for the man. "Sounds like you're in a bit of a pickle there, mate! You probably know all the flying stats, so I'll spare you all that crap. Have you tried a good shot of whisky to calm the nerves? My old man swore by it... but then, he does swear a lot... plus, he's an alcoholic... so... he drank a shitload of whisky... while swearing...." *Charlotte, you dufus, just stop talking, you're not helping here.*

The man's shoulders relaxed slightly, and he slowly turned to look at Charlotte. A small smile melted into a larger smile, then a chuckle, then laughter. As if by magic, the turbulence calmed quickly, and the seatbelt sign was switched off again.

"Thank you, Miss. I'm sorry, I'm usually not this rude. I am, as you said, in a 'pickle.'" He sighed. "Thanks for making me laugh... it hasn't happened in a while."

"Any time! Well, any time during the next couple of hours, anyway. The flight chicky is coming this way; I'll get us a couple of drinks. What do you feel like?"

"Hard liquor. Or a cocktail please. It's what I *would* have been drinking on Hamilton Island, had I stayed and followed my itinerary."

Charlotte nodded and extracted the menu from the seat pouch in front.

"Done! Excuse me," she said, calling over the flight attendant, who nodded and smiled.

"What can I do for you?"

"Could we get a couple of scotch and tonics? My mate here

doesn't like the bumps, and I've always wanted to try one! You'd think I would have tried everything, having worked in a bar."

"Thanks again, Miss, I think I can finally unclench my fists now," he said, wiping his hands on his thighs. "My name is Jacob, or Jake. What's yours?"

"Charlotte. And you're welcome, Jacob or Jake!" she beamed, shaking his still-clammy hand enthusiastically.

He laughed again.

"Jake is fine. I'll let you get back to your movie now. I heard you mutter 'yay' before when you found the one you wanted."

"Oh, *Fire Night*? I love action movies and horror—the gorier and scarier, the better! I just got a make-up artist job in Hollywood, so can't wait to work on these kinds of sets."

Jake's face lit up and he took a breath as if about to share a big secret, but as he did, a tall, bronzed and slender woman approached along the aisle towards their seats. Simultaneously, the flight attendant arrived from the opposite direction with their drinks.

"Ahh, so you're doing pretty well I see, Jacob," the woman smiled sweetly, looking at Charlotte and then to the drinks, raising her sculpted eyebrows. Jake handed a drink to Charlotte and took one for himself.

"Charlotte here was just cheering me up, Meg... that turbulence was *rough*."

The elegant woman nodded and leaned forward; her flawless skin shimmered and thick, black lashes contrasted beautifully against her sparkling almond eyes.

"I've managed to get us some seats together in business class," said Meg. "One of the flight attendants went to college with my agent... we'd better go before someone else takes them."

Jake gasped with the news, then looked disappointed as he turned to look at a smiling Charlotte.

"There you go, matey!" she said, elbowing him gently in the arm. "Your luck's turning around! Business class, smooth ride, beautiful lady and a fancy bevvy in your hand!"

"You are a ray of sunshine, Charlotte. It was lovely to meet you, good luck in Hollywood—it's a small town, I am certain we'll see each other again!" He grabbed his belongings and left.

Charlotte farewelled the pair, then realised she could now move across one seat to the aisle, creating more room for the cramped foursome occupying the middle row. She moved the few things she'd taken out of her backpack, found the movie again, reclined her seat and made herself comfy.

Returning to the moment as she stepped into the shower, she was still thinking about her encounter with Jake. *I wonder how he is doing after that long flight... and what it is he does in Hollywood? No matter, I've got enough to think about right now!*

After her shower, Charlotte dressed in skinny black jeans and the black uniform top she'd collected at reception and pulled her hair back in a sleek bun. After applying her simple makeup, she stood back and studied her appearance. *Not bad for a little girl from Gundagai.* She grabbed her keys, phone, backpack and a light jacket before closing the door behind her. The morning air was slightly chilly although the sun shone with the promise of another warm and pleasant day. Charlotte suspected this kind of weather was what she'd expect in Hollywood, and why so many people flocked to the state. *Although we do get this kind of weather in Gundagai, without the bloody smog...*

Looking at the email from her boss, Amanda Voss, on her phone and the directions on how to get to the studio, Charlotte wondered what sort of person she'd be like to work for. During the Zoom meeting, Amanda was among a few other key people and executives who had interviewed her. Amanda had remained quiet, sporting a sour-looking expression for the duration of the meeting. Charlotte's instructor at the Sydney academy had mentioned she could be difficult, but it would be an amazing learning experience. Charlotte had a feeling about her but shrugged it off as nerves. Besides, if the job was terrible, she'd only have to put up with it for a year while her working visa was valid. How bad could it be?

After reporting to security and obtaining her pass, Charlotte followed the narrow roads that wormed their way through the maze of buildings, periodically looking down at her phone to check the map she'd been given. Building G was right ahead of her, next to a small patch of grass and a solitary tree. A spike of homesickness hit Charlotte in the stomach, along with a pop of nerves. *It'll be fine, Char... just remember who you are. Hey, that rhymes.* With a smirk, Charlotte opened the door labelled 'Building G' and walked inside.

Although she was twenty minutes early, there was already bustling activity inside the cavernous space. The dark ceiling was barely visible above the numerous steel beams and cords running along it. Technical equipment was being moved and assembled, a few harried people carrying glittery costumes rushed past, barely glancing at Charlotte, who stood gaping, taking it all in. Her eyes wandered through the different groups of people attending to different tasks, then found a small group gathered inside one of the smaller rooms off to the side. Through the open door, she could see mirrors and prosthetic masks hanging loosely from what could have been a line of severed heads on a table. *Ahh, the make-up crew! I bet that's them!*

Taking a deep breath, Charlotte took a step towards the room and instantly collided with a large blunt object. Regaining her balance and rubbing her arm from the side-on impact, she turned and yelled with fright as a giant horse's head stared back at her. The crew member carrying the prop had fallen over and was now sprawled on the floor with the animal's hooves and a leg scattered around him. Charlotte reached out her hand and offered to help the man up.

"Hey, stop *horsing* around, young man, you could have really *clopped* me," she said with a sly grin.

The young man took her hand but once on his feet, almost immediately dropped back to the floor to pick everything up.

"Sorry, Miss," he said, hurrying away awkwardly with the props, looking like he needed at least two more sets of hands. She rubbed her now throbbing arm, thinking her puns at least warranted acknowledgement—or checking to see if she was okay out of human courtesy. Reorienting herself, she continued towards what she believed to be her destination. As Charlotte arrived at the doorway, she smiled and saw a handful of disinterested-looking people dotted around the room. A squat, middle-aged lady stood in front who looked vaguely familiar. Her long, silver grey hair cascaded down her narrow shoulders, and her manicured hands tapped impatiently on her portly hips. She turned to address Charlotte, her expression poised as if to launch into a tirade.

"Hey, folks, is this the make-up team?" Charlotte asked while waving. She looked around the room, eliciting a couple of sneers and judgemental head-to-toe glances. A lean black lady with short, braided hair and high cheekbones smiled warmly at Charlotte. *Hey, I got a smile from someone!*

"Ah, you're finally here," said the lady up front in a tone that would freeze water. "Everyone, this is our new girl, Charlotte Grin, all the way from Australia. Say hello to the fresh meat!"

"It's Charlotte Grant, but I do grin a lot! Am I late? The email said eight thir-"

"We always start at eight, Charlotte," the lady cut in condescendingly.

Charlotte smiled but it morphed into a straight face when she recognised the lady.

"I'm Amanda Voss, the director of the make-up contracting company here. You met me during your interview. Please take a seat and I'll continue from where you interrupted me."

Charlotte grimaced and sat down on the sofa next to the nice lady who shuffled over.

Amanda cleared her throat dramatically and made her way to the door, slamming it shut. She flicked her hair, then slowly walked back to where she'd been standing.

"As I was saying, during the filming of this sci-fi series, there will be a mix of offsite-based work and filming here in the studio. This is a project with lots of prosthetics, and a slew of extras. It's going to be hard work. The majority of the creation will be done by us, however, there will be some studio employees coming in on some of the scenes. Conceptualisation has been done, but we will have some creative allowances. All up, it should take between nine to twelve months to film, then the reshoot period. Because of your gross incompetence and budget cuts, you'll notice there are several teammates not here, having been fired."

Charlotte subtly looked around the room and saw only cool expressions on the array of faces that made up the team.

"We lost big time on the last film we completed and didn't even get a nomination. I will not allow your collective ineptitude to rob us of another award. It has to be faster, better, more stunning. No more goofing around and wasting time—I'm not running a charity, clear? As it is, we'll have to bring Charlotte up to speed and waste extra time on training her, so breaks will be minimal. Tess, you'll be showing her the ropes."

Charlotte glanced sideways at Tess and smiled apologetically.

Amanda continued for what seemed like forever, lecturing the team about what not to do. Charlotte struggled to follow all the terms and references made by her new boss but was certain there wasn't a single utterance of praise in there or any kind of positive direction. *All stick and no carrot...*

Once she'd finished the tirade, during which there were a number of audible sighs, Charlotte turned to Tess and whispered, "Hey Tess, nice to meet you! I'm a fast learner, so hopefully you'll get your breaks back soon."

Tess took Charlotte's outstretched hand and shook it gently with a weary smile. "Hey, Charlotte, nice to meet you, too. It's all good, we're used to tough conditions."

Charlotte opened her mouth to ask Tess more questions when she was again interrupted by Amanda's sharp voice.

"Tess, why are you two sitting there? I instructed you to show Charlotte the ropes—we've got a big day ahead and I don't want her making more mistakes than you have the capacity to clean up!"

They rose in response, and Tess beckoned Charlotte to follow her out the door.

"We'll start with the safety tour first," Tess said blankly as Charlotte smiled at Amanda's ominous face, scrutinising them as they left. As they entered the busy main building, Charlotte whistled.

"Holy guacamole! Is Amanda always so... so... such a...?" Charlotte said, struggling to find the right description.

"Is she always such a bitch?" Tess replied. "Yeah girl, she is. You just gotta let it slide—I've been working with Amanda the longest now, two years. She doesn't keep contractors for long, but witnessing that, I'm sure you can see why. How long you with us?"

"My visa is for a year, but they said it has the possibility of being extended."

Tess looked back and wrinkled her nose.

"That could be a slight issue. If she knows she's got you tied into a contract, her behaviour could get worse. Do you have thick skin, Charlotte?"

"Well, I got bitten by a redback spider once and lived to tell the tale."

"Hmm... that's pretty impressive. But Amanda Voss is a different kind of spider, honey. She bites, too, and her venom has a lasting impact." Tess winked.

Charlotte decided at that moment she really, really liked Tess.

The next few hours were spent glued to Tess's side, figuring out where to go for what and when. It was a lot of information to absorb, but Charlotte was determined to learn more quickly than usual, so as not to be a burden on her team. She met a lot of people, and stuck her head into a lot of rooms, cupboards and storage spaces. Tess assured Charlotte that if she forgot anything, she was more than welcome to ask, which Charlotte appreciated. As she sat and watched Tess carefully preparing a prosthetic piece for one of the lead actor's faces, Charlotte could feel eyes on her. She turned, and sure enough saw Amanda staring, then beckoning her forward. *Oh God, what now... was I standing the wrong way or something?*

"Charlotte. How are you settling in, finding everything okay?" she asked with a forced calm tone and teeth bared in what could have been a smile. Now she was closer, Charlotte examined her boss. Amanda's makeup was plastered thick over a completely hairless face—the harsh lines drawn around her eyes and mouth reminded Charlotte of the band *The Kiss*.

"Thanks, Amanda, I think-"

"That's great, so before you go any further, there's a follow-up rule that's not 'technically' a rule...." She winked. "... It's called: 'you don't screw the crew.' You have any kind of sexual or romantic relationship with anyone to do with work and it's an instant dismissal. No dating, no consorting outside of work. 'K?"

Charlotte opened her mouth to say something but was cut off once more.

"Trust me, it's much easier this way. You're pretty and completely ignorant to how this industry works. I've seen whole sets, whole movie projects, closed down because of jilted lovers. It's bad for business, and this is *my* business. My house, my rules. 'K?" Without waiting for a response, Amanda patted Charlotte's arm and yelled after someone she wanted to speak with.

Puffing out her cheeks as she processed this information, Charlotte returned to Tess's side.

"Hey, girl, what did you think of all that?" she asked quietly as she continued her work. "You still wanna stay in Hollywood and work for the meanest troll under the bridge?"

"She certainly seems like a... *strong* woman... hells bells!" Charlotte responded as the two watched Amanda networking and squawking with some people in suits who had just arrived.

Tess snorted. "Yeah, that's one way to describe her. Hey, there's a few of us going to the bar later after work, wanna come with? We can talk a little easier there."

"Are we allowed to, Tess? Does that constitute 'consorting' outside of work, is that off-limits?" Charlotte narrowed her eyes. "Plus, I don't think the rest of those guys like me very much. I've got the impression a couple of times today they're laughing at me behind my back."

"Tonight isn't dating, honey, it's just drinks for people who need to blow off steam. The 'screw the crew' rule is definitely one of her deal breakers, but this ain't it. I've seen her though, screamin' like a giant beet, going ballistic at two of her contractors she caught holding hands... and because she knows everyone in Hollywood, she uses that as a threat to keep us in line. I think it's just because she's jealous and hasn't been laid in decades. And don't worry about the crew, they're bitchy to anyone new, especially if they're nice. I think you should come with."

Charlotte thought about it. It would be nice to hang out and get to know her new colleagues a little better.

"Sure, I'm in," she said, smiling at Tess, who nodded and patted her on the arm.

"Good. 'Cos I got a babysitter and I ain't losin' that opportunity! Plus, we'll all need alcohol by the end of today—trust me!"

CHAPTER 4

By Friday, Charlotte was starting to feel the fatigue induced by her surroundings. Never one to pretend she was someone else, or something other than she was, the lack of authenticity she felt with Hollywood culture was proving exhausting.

'Voss the Boss,' whom she'd received several warnings about throughout the week, had thankfully left her alone so far. Charlotte stuck to Tess like glue and was enjoying her new colleague's company in such a tense environment.

Apparently, Amanda always acted in the same way with new team members; mostly sweet to begin with, then the façade quickly faded, and her true colours would appear. Charlotte knew she needed to last a year for visa purposes, so figured if she could avoid her boss and keep as busy as possible, her working day could be easier.

As it was the end of the week, Charlotte indulged in a takeaway coffee, a luxury she'd not be able to afford every day in Hollywood.

The café she wanted to try was one she passed each morning. It was bustling inside with exhausted-looking staff carrying trays and armed with clipboards and tablets, while outside, beautiful people took their time smiling with their impossibly straight teeth, chatting and extending their bejewelled hands out to sip their morning beverages. Neatly trimmed trees without a leaf out of place, fancy wrought-iron furniture with trim-lined cushions and large black awnings were arranged outside on the wide sidewalk. A well-worn phrase repeating in Charlotte's mind came to the fore again... *we're not in Gundagai anymore, Toto.*

Approaching the entrance, she quickly stepped out of the way as a harried young man in thick glasses approached the door from the inside. He was juggling a tray of six coffees, a little paper bag with the cafes' brand on the side, and a stack of tablets and clipboards in the other arm. Charlotte smiled at the youngster and ensured the door was open wide enough for him to pass by holding it open awkwardly with one arm. The man's face contorted with confusion as he looked at Charlotte's gesture.

"You look like you need an extra arm there, matey!" she said to the bespeckled youngster. Instead of saying thank you or reciprocating a smile, the youngster's eyes widened, then quickly averted from Charlotte's face, somehow making himself smaller and faster as he sped out the door. He reminded Charlotte of a little hamster, wearing tiny horn-rimmed glasses on a little wheel... *must go faster.* She blew her cheeks out at his rude reaction and made her way to the back of the small line leading to the counter. Charlotte heard a loud chuckle behind her in the queue.

"Not quite the reaction you're used to, eh Miss?" said a gentle voice.

Charlotte turned and saw a tall, immaculately dressed man with dark salt-and-pepper hair, deep blue eyes and a warm smile.

"Yeah... where I'm from, everyone knows everyone. You'd never behave like that, or your mum would find out, then you'd be in bloody big trouble!"

The man laughed. "Well, you can trust me at least, Miss. I'd never behave like that. Plus, I don't make anyone get me coffee. I'm not that important."

Charlotte smiled, moved forward in the queue, then turned back around to face him. "You seem nice, and that's the main thing. I don't care about names or job titles. It's who you are as a person, not how famous you are that counts."

"You are too kind. Well, even if you don't care what my name is, I'm Edward Meeks. I've been a local for a long while now. Where are you from, kid?" he asked.

Charlotte took his offered hand and shook it enthusiastically. *Finally, a friendly face.*

"I'm Charlotte Grant. You can call me Char. I don't reckon you'll know where I'm from, Sir, so I'll just say Australia."

"Oh God, honey, you definitely don't need to call me Sir. I don't deserve such a title. Call me Meeks, like everyone else does. Hey, Char, you're up." He pointed behind her.

Charlotte turned and stepped up to the counter, narrowing her eyes as she read the drinks on offer. The server greeted her perfunctorily, and after a few moments breathed audibly through their nose as her confusion started to peak.

I just want one with milk, one without.... What the hell do all these things mean? She glanced at the African American server's nametag pinned at chest-level, which read 'Sam,' then up to their now glaring eyes. *I don't know whether Sam is a 'mate' or a 'miss'... shit!*

"Hi, mate... miss... sorry... um... I just want a white one and a big, long black... do you have one of those...?" Sam's mouth, along with several other servers who had been busily working behind the counter, stopped and gaped at her. *Shit. Maybe long blacks mean something else here...*

There was a chuckle behind her, which seemed to be the only sound echoing through the cavernous faux pas she'd just committed. A hand gently wrapped around Charlotte's left shoulder and a calming male voice spoke to her right.

"Hey, Sam, my friend from Australia here would just like an Americano and a Café au lait. I'll just have my usual, thank you."

Charlotte saw his hand extend to pay with his phone. Sam sneered at Charlotte and held out the machine for Meeks to tap. Charlotte wrinkled her nose and moved quickly to the small but elegantly decorated waiting area. She furrowed her brow and looked at Meeks.

"Oh my God... Meeks! Thank you so much. That was... that was..."

"Awkward as hell, that's what that was," he said, laughing and reaching to return his phone to the back pocket of his jeans. "Haven't you explored any Hollywood cafes yet?"

"Nah. I literally landed last weekend, and it's been all-go at work. Plus, at these prices, on my salary...."

"Ahh, I get it. Well, you've got a guide now, kid. I'm at your service, whenever you need me to get you out of embarrassing coffee situations or just show you the good food places. Are you a foodie?"

Charlotte gasped. "Yes! Well, I'm an L-plater, but I love trying new food! Last time I went to Sydney I tried–"

"Meeks," said one of the baristas and held out a holder with three coffees.

Meeks thanked the barista and took his coffee from the tray before handing it to Charlotte.

She tilted her head and thanked him again. "Are you sure I can't give you some money for these? I feel bad, you don't even know me."

"It's who you are as a person that counts," he said with a smile and winked as he reached into his pocket and pulled out a business card. "Here is my cell. When you're settled and you want to go try some weird-ass Californian cuisine, give me a call, okay?" He glanced over her head at the window. "Ahh, I've gotta go, my 7:30 is out there... and he looks a little cranky. It was lovely to meet you, have a great day, Char." He patted her on the arm and moved quickly but gracefully to the door. Charlotte waved after him. As she bent down to pick up her bag on the floor, she heard sniggers from behind the counter and thought she heard the comment 'Forrest Gump.'

"Thank you all so much for being so understanding and welcoming to an outsider!" she said with feigned sweetness to the counter staff, waving again more enthusiastically. "I just hope y'all have a super great day!" She turned towards the door with her coffees in hand.

Bunch of snooty pricks...

She made her way back out again into the slightly brisk spring morning and crossed the street, heading towards the studio. A man selling star maps was setting up on a corner, and various shopkeepers along Sunset Boulevard were preparing for their day. Charlotte enjoyed strolling along and staring in the windows of the fancy shops and looking at what shows were on. She wondered what it was like to ever meet one of the celebrities that had a star and was careful never to walk on them. *Somehow it feels disrespectful, like walking on someone's grave...*

Although Charlotte didn't officially start work until 8:30 am, she had always preferred to arrive early so she could settle in. "Always better to be ten minutes early, than ten minutes late," as her dad used to say. One of his better sayings, and one he'd actually adhere to. Especially when it involved happy hour at the pub.

Charlotte made her way through the front boom gates of the studio, saying good morning to the elderly man who worked the morning shift. He was also a cheery chap and seeing him first thing in the morning would boost Charlotte's spirits.

"Good morning, Sir Gus, and how is your kingdom on this lovely Friday?" Charlotte asked, a question that was becoming a staple in their royalty-themed dialogue.

Gus chuckled and tipped his cap at her.

"Just fine, thank you, Lady Charlotte! May you have a day as gallant as your good self!"

Charlotte laughed and curtseyed at the guard before carrying on towards her destination. She couldn't remember what started their friendly banter but was greatly enjoying their morning interactions.

As she made her way through the open door of the deserted recording building, what she'd been referring to as 'the tractor shed,' Charlotte saw a man bent over a fold-up table at the far end of the room. He was leaning on the top of its crumpled frame, hands resting on his bent knees, head hung low. As she slowly approached, it looked as if he was shuddering. *Is that guy crying?* Charlotte decided to scuff her heels subtly to announce her presence.

"Hey... mate, are you okay? Do you need a hand?"

The man was startled and quickly turned to the wall, wiping his face with his sleeve. Charlotte wasn't sure whether to leave him be or stay put, but something told her to stay.

"Do you need a tissue? Pollen count is pretty bad today I hear!" She put the coffee tray down on the ground and extracted a little pack of tissues from her backpack. She took one and reached around to the man's front so he could take it without turning around. He smelled *good*.

"You're very kind, thank you," said the man quietly with a thick, gravelly Spanish accent. She waited awkwardly as he blew his nose; she heard him take a deep breath before turning around.

Although his eyes were red and puffy, they locked with Charlotte's... and she felt everything go quiet. It was as if everything around his face was sparkling: his tanned skin, dark brown eyes and a dark stubble to match the colour of his dishevelled wavy hair that hung haphazardly over his brow. He stared right back at her. Time had somehow stopped. The man cleared his throat, and Charlotte quickly closed her mouth, suddenly realising it had been wide open.

"Hi... um... you... hi, uh, are you new here?" he stuttered, his gaze sinking to the floor.

"Yep, yep that's me. The new girl! Straight off the boat from Australia. How are you? Shit, obviously not great... and now I've sworn at you... 'cussed' as you Yanks say... not that you sound like a Yank... um... no, that's not what I meant." Charlotte closed her eyes and took a deep breath. She then opened them and smiled at the man, now chuckling. "Okay! I'm going to stop talking now."

"Please don't do that. I think that's the first I've laughed in years." Charlotte furrowed her brow.

"Is it because of the table?" The man threw back his head and laughed loudly.

"I wish... fold-up tables are slightly easier than messy divorces."

Ah. The poor guy... the poor, ridiculously handsome guy that is possibly the most gorgeous creature I've ever seen with a voice like velvet and eyes like... like...

"Oh, right. I'm sorry, mate. Is there anything I can do to help?"

The man looked at her quizzically, smiling slightly as he cocked his head. "You're really not from here, are you, Miss? You're way too considerate and kind to be from this town." Their eyes burned together for a moment, then Charlotte snorted as she laughed.

"I do tend to stick out like dog's balls."

Shit... Charlotte, you idiot, stop talking, stop talking NOW!

He laughed again, then held out his hand.

"My name is Antonio. What's your name?"

She smiled and took his hand, which enveloped hers.

"Charlotte. Nice to meet you! So, what do you do around here, Antonio?" Unwillingly, she let go of his hand, realising she'd now been shaking it a little longer than socially acceptable.

He had a crooked smile on his face and paused briefly, as if weighing up how to answer.

"I, uh... I'm kind of... well, instead of the dog's balls, I'm the dog's body. I do a little bit of everything."

"Ahh, so you'd be one of the irreplaceable people then... the ones we can't do without," she said playfully, giving him a little wink.

"Well, maybe... that's probably debatable..." he responded, looking at his feet and smiling sheepishly.

An idea popped into Charlotte's head. "Hey, I got a coffee this morning, but I reckon you need it more than me. Do you like coffee? Milk or no milk?" She leaned down to pick up the coffee tray.

Antonio stuttered and put a hand on his chest. "Charlotte, you are so kind. I... well, I love coffee. Black coffee is how I take it. My assist... uh, my friend... was going to grab me one on his way in, but I guess he's running late. I'm sure he'll be here soon. Please don't give up yours for me."

"It's all good, Antonio, you have this one. I'll be fine." She passed him the drink, their fingers touching briefly when he accepted it. Charlotte felt a little spark connecting them, making her flinch.

He looked at the coffee as he took it, then back at her earnestly.

"You are... thank you. Thank you so much, Charlotte. You are like... sunshine." She felt her legs weaken as she looked into his eyes. Realising she was now blatantly staring, Charlotte snapped herself out of her trance and bent down shakily to pick up her bag and the remaining coffee.

"Well, Antonio, I gotta run. It was so lovely to meet you. I really hope your day gets better. As my dad always used to say, 'this too shall pass.'"

Antonio smiled at her intently.

"Charlotte... thank you again for brightening my day. Oh, which department are you in? Where are you working?"

"Makeup! I'm working for Amanda in makeup and prosthetics".

"Oh, Amanda. Okay. I hope you are enjoying it there... let me know if... well, let me know if you run into any trouble. We want to keep people like you."

"No worries, mate, will do! See ya!" Charlotte attempted a casual wave, but by doing so spilled hot coffee over her hand. She turned to hide the pain registering on her face and walked towards the door leading to the make-up room. Her legs were still trembling and she desperately hoped if he was still watching her that her lack of coordination wouldn't be noticeable.

Should I look back? Nah. What if he's not looking, and I'll look even more idiotic and desperate? Ahh, what the hell...

A few steps before reaching the open door, she turned her head. Antonio was looking right at her. She waved and smiled, which he reciprocated. Passing through the doorway, her trembling free hand fumbled for the light switch, which slowly flickered and illuminated the huge room. She strode over to the doorway of the smaller staffroom and again turned on the lights, threw her bag and coffee on the counter and collapsed onto the couch in the corner. Her heart was still pounding, her eyes wide and what felt like pure electricity pulsing through her. *How am I supposed to concentrate on work now? I couldn't apply makeup with these hands, the cast would look like they got shot with a bloody clown gun.*

Unaware of how long she'd been sitting there daydreaming, Charlotte was startled when three of her coworkers walked through the door. Tess gave Charlotte a little wink as she took off her sunglasses and placed her bag under the counter.

"Good morning! Tess, I got you a coffee. Sorry, guys, I didn't realise you'd be here today, or I would have got you all coffees, too."

Tess looked at the drink on the counter and smiled at Charlotte while the other two just looked confused at the gesture.

"Girl, you are too nice, thank you! Where's yours? You didn't just stop to get me one, did you?"

Charlotte leaned forward eagerly; she had to tell someone about her recent encounter.

"I did, but I gave it to this guy, Antonio. We were chatting; apparently, he's having a tough time right now. I gave him a tissue. Oh my God, Tess, he's so gorgeous. He seemed really sad, so I gave him my coffee."

Tess had covered her mouth with her hand and the others gaped at her.

Charlotte's eyes widened as she looked between them, frowning at their reactions.

"What...? What did I do? Why are you all staring at me?"

It was Zephyr, the more flamboyant of her lesser-known colleagues, who answered first.

"Antonio *Sanchez*? A little taller than you, dark hair, voice you'd die for?"

"Yeah...? And he said he was going through a divorce or something...?" Charlotte answered nervously. Her three colleagues laughed incredulously, exchanging looks like it was a big deal. She looked at Tess's face, now wrinkling her nose slightly. What terrible social blunder had she committed this time?

"What is he, like, the cleaner?"

Laughter erupted.

"Honey, do you watch movies in Australia? Like, you know, the multi-billion-dollar industry you're working in?"

Charlotte stared blankly as Zephyr put a hand on their hip and leaned closer. "Antonio is the fucking *director*."

CHAPTER 5

Charlotte froze. "He's... the *what?*"

"The D-I-R-E-C-T-O-R," Zephyr mouthed loudly. "He never talks to *anyone*. Let alone someone so far down the food chain."

Charlotte was so shocked she didn't care to react to their condescension.

Tess cooed and walked over to sit beside her on the couch. "Hey, don't worry about it, honey. From what I hear, he's an understanding guy. It sounds like you two got along really well." She bumped her shoulder gently against Charlotte's.

"He was so nice... and really down to earth.... Why didn't he just tell me? Oh man, I feel like such an *idiot...* '*what do you do around here, Antonio?*'" Charlotte mocked, head now in her hands.

"Aww, you'll be okay, girl. We're going to be so busy over the next couple of weeks that I'm sure you'll forget all about it. Plus, Amanda will be around today doing some PR work apparently... not that those two descriptions should be in the same sentence, but anyway.... Let's split my coffee between us and we can get started on setting up for the day. Sound okay?"

Charlotte nodded resignedly and stood up. How on earth she wouldn't be thinking about this for the foreseeable future was beyond her right now, but Tess was probably right. Especially if Amanda was around, she'd need her head in the game.

But Tess wasn't 'probably' right; she was one hundred percent right. Not long after they'd started working with the cast members, Amanda arrived. With a face like thunder, she stormed into the make-up room, barking orders and issuing rhetorical questions.

"Why am I paying you all so much? All of these masks need to be finished; they look like they've been painted by goddamned kindergarteners! Why are we still working on the base colours when filming has already started?"

Charlotte looked around surreptitiously from the actor she was currently working with to see what her other colleagues were doing. Zephyr was finishing up with a main cast member who now had a massive life-like gash across his face; it looked amazing. Glancing over at Tess, who caught her eye and pulled a face behind Amanda's back, she noted her work looked incredible.

Wow, she's so talented... they all are. I still can't believe I'm in this room...

Charlotte looked back to her own work critically, checking out different angles to see whether she'd met the brief. The male cast member, who looked vaguely familiar to Charlotte, looked up from his phone and smiled at her.

"What do you think, Miss, am I ready to get out there and kick some alien ass?" he asked, mimicking guns with his fingers.

"Yeah, I reckon you'd win hands down, mate—go give 'em hell, okay?"

"Will do. You've done a fantastic job. You're new, yeah?"

"Sure am. And thank you for the compliment!" Charlotte was about to ask the man's name when she looked up and saw Amanda talking to Antonio. He was in costume and looking like he was heading in her direction. *Shit!*

The actor turned in his chair, saw who Charlotte was looking at and chuckled.

"Ahh, okay. Enough chit-chat. I'd better clear the chair for the director's ass, since he's leading our alien campaign." He rose from his chair.

Double shit.

"No, you're right, mate, sorry I didn't mean to be rude. I was just gauging how many cast members we have left to prep. You're all good, no rush!" She tried to appear calm when she felt anything but. Amanda was now pointing Antonio in the direction of her chair. Charlotte smiled, shook the hand of the departing actor and bounded over to Tess.

"Tess, I really have to pee. Plus, I really don't want to have to work with Antonio. I will literally die from embarrassment. Can you please help me?"

Tess chuckled as she nodded to the actor currently in her chair, signalling they were finished.

"Okay, girl, you go pee. Then on your way back, go check with Gerome, the guy with the orange baseball cap, see if anyone needs touch-ups. We should have done that already, but we're so short staffed today. I'll run interference—go!"

"I adore you, Tess—I'm naming my first born after you."

Tess laughed and pushed her gently towards the side door. "Go!"

Looking straight down so as not to make eye contact with anyone, Charlotte tucked some stray hair strands behind her ear and tried to casually blend in with the surroundings. She heard Amanda laughing loudly, though it sounded a little forced, and Tess welcoming Antonio as she made her escape out the back door.

Feeling relieved after her speedy bathroom visit, although a little light-headed from a lack of food, Charlotte did as Tess suggested and quickly sought out Gerome on the filming floor. She was extremely glad Tess had mentioned his orange baseball cap; it was impossible for a new person to know where to go or whom to talk to. Everyone was busy, usually holding a clipboard or iPad, and almost everyone wore a puffer vest. It was like an impeccably dressed army directing another completely filthy army of alien-hunters.

"Excuse me, Gerome? Hi, I'm Charlotte, one of the new make-up artists. Do you guys need any help from us on the floor?"

"Ahh, Charlotte, hello, nice to meet you." he said warmly, smiling as he shook Charlotte's hand. "We did need you guys earlier but we're okay now, thank you though."

"Cool, just checking. I'll let you get back to it!"

"Thank you, and your team is doing an amazing job, we're getting some amazing shots today," he said.

Charlotte stood next to him for a moment, watching everyone prepare for the next scene.

"So, Miss, it looks like we're winning..." came a familiar voice behind her.

Charlotte turned to see the actor she'd previously worked on in the make-up chair. Startled slightly by his appearance since he genuinely looked like he'd been in battle, Charlotte laughed.

"Yay, go you!" she said, performing an instinctive high-five with the young man. "Thanks for representing humanity! How do you feel?"

He sighed and held up a can of soda as if he was doing product placement. "It's not over yet. There's a pause in the fight so we can make use of corporate beverage sponsorship." he said.

"Hey, even aliens can't compete with a cold blast of vanilla refreshment."

"That's absolutely right. Hey, if we die today, can I at least know your name?"

"I guess it would help knowing the little people you saved... I'm Charlotte Grant."

"Liam Reeves. And you're not 'little,' you're super important. Who could make a useless wimp of an actor like me look like I've actually accomplished something?" He gestured at his outfit.

Oh my God... it's Liam Reeves. The mega-star, the actor I've drooled over countless times on the screen and in magazines...

"Liam Reeves... oh my goodness..." she blurted, hand on her heart. "I didn't recognise you! Wow! It's great to meet you properly. I'm a huge fan! You made me cry!"

Liam's face fell. "Oh no, what did I do?" he asked earnestly.

"Your wife died, then you said all that amazing, inspirational stuff to your daughter... mate... I went through like a carton of tissues during *Wonderstuff*."

"Ahh, yes, I do get that a lot... kinda wish I had a tissue sponsor too. I'd still like to make it up to you though. A few of us are going to a bar tonight, that dive around the corner. Can I buy you a drink?"

Before she had time to sort out the conflicting thoughts his question generated, a hand grabbed her arm roughly, tugging her sideways.

"*What* are you *doing* out here!" Amanda yelled inches from her face.

Momentarily thrown off balance, Charlotte's eyes widened as she steadied herself. She glanced sideways to see Liam's concerned expression before turning forward to look at her boss's fuming face, which had turned a deep rouge.

"Charlotte just checked in with Gerome, Amanda, we needed you guys earlier," Liam called out. "She was just on her way back when I had some questions for her."

Charlotte saw Amanda's teeth in what could have been a smile directed at Liam as she dragged Charlotte back towards the make-up room. *Oh crap, crap. I'm in trouble...*

"Don't you ever, *ever*, leave your make-up chair unless I give you explicit instructions to do so... got it?" she hissed.

"I had to pee. On my way back from the toilet, I checked in—I've only been gone for like two min—"

"I don't care how long you've been gone for, you *idiot*. You never leave your chair unless I tell you to. Especially when I'm sending the *director of the goddamned movie* over to you. I looked ridiculous, and he didn't know why you suddenly ran off. Do you understand? Can your tiny Australian brain comprehend what I'm saying?"

Charlotte took a deep breath. She could swim against this current, or with it.

"I'm sorry, Amanda. I'll check with you before I go to the bathroom next time. Please can you refrain from insulting me and where I come from. And please can you let go of my arm, you're hurting me." She stared straight into her boss's narrowed eyes with a cold, detached look and held her withering gaze.

Amanda looked at her hand and released her vice-like grip.

Charlotte maintained steady eye contact, rubbing her arm and wincing slightly. Not waiting for a response, Charlotte walked calmly back towards the make-up room.

She had to admit that this encounter had rattled her. No stranger to conflict, violence or physical rough-housing from various life experiences, especially from working in a pub, Charlotte hadn't expected this level of treatment from an employer—especially here.

I guess this is why they were desperate for staff... choosing to ship over a little girl from Gundagai... no-one who knows Amanda Voss wants to work with that bloody cow.

Tess caught sight of Charlotte as she strode back into the busy make-up room, looking at the arm Charlotte was still rubbing. Tess's mouth fell open, and she quickly excused herself from Antonio still sitting in her chair.

He smiled broadly at Charlotte, who reciprocated, albeit weakly.

"Oh my God, honey, are you okay?" she whispered. "Amanda stormed out of here after you. I hope I didn't get you into trouble... and what happened to your arm?"

Charlotte could feel Antonio watching; this wasn't the time to be forthright.

"It's fine, Tess, it's all good," Charlotte said with the biggest smile she could muster. "At least I've peed." She chuckled.

Tess looked unconvinced by her nonchalant response. Out of the corner of her eye, Charlotte saw Antonio leaning forward. *Is he eavesdropping?*

"Those look like big, red finger marks... shit, and nail marks," Tess whispered discreetly, looking at Charlotte's arm and back at her face as if trying to picture what had just occurred.

"Tess, it's okay. I'll tell you later. We've got loads to get through. We'll go to the bar later, okay?"

"First round is on me, girl," she said, furrowing her brow and lightly patting Charlotte's uninjured arm.

As Charlotte walked back to her chair, she could feel Antonio's eyes upon her. Choosing not to engage and still feeling a little shaken, Charlotte needed to focus. The embarrassment she'd felt earlier was now magnified tenfold.

How on earth can I ever look Antonio in the eye again?

But that didn't matter right now. Taking a deep breath in front of her chair, she looked up at the line of actors and with a wide smile, beckoned the next one forward.

Luckily, the make-up team didn't see much of Amanda for the rest of the day. How behaving like that with Charlotte in front of the cast and crew was 'good PR,' Charlotte would never know.

It was nearly 6pm, and after working for ten hours' straight, the crew were all feeling it. Tess had told Charlotte in the afternoon she'd overheard Gerome talking to Amanda. Apparently, he'd never seen make-up effects this good, and the results they were achieving were "outstanding." Charlotte wondered whether these compliments and acknowledgement would ever be passed on to the team directly, however, knowing Amanda, she suspected this would be all the positive reinforcement they would receive.

"Okay, team, I'm calling it. We're done. They've finished filming for the day, and we all need a drink." Tess threw a cloth onto her chair. She received a chorus of groans in reply.

Charlotte stood up from the prosthetics cabinet she'd been cleaning and stretched, feeling some bones crack in her body's response to the gruelling shift.

"Ten minutes and we're outta here," said Tess. "Let's get everything ready for tomorrow, real quick!"

Despite the fatigue hanging in the room, the small team sprung into action, cleaning brushes, wiping down their chairs, sweeping the floor. In just over eight minutes, the room was neatly organised, and the crew members had their bags in hand.

As they switched off the lights and headed out into the balmy Californian twilight, Tess put her arm around Charlotte's waist while they walked, hanging back behind the others.

"Charlotte, honey, today was a tough one. I'm really sorry you got into trouble with our bitch of a boss. Please know I didn't do that on purpose... I'm not *that* person. There's a lot of backstabbing in this town, but I promise you, that's not me. We honestly needed someone on the floor, so I thought it would be a perfect opportunity for you to do that. I'm so sorry you got the wrath of the dragon." Tess squeezed Charlotte gently, a gesture that hinted at forgiveness.

"Aww, Tess, I didn't think for a second you'd done it on purpose! I thought you were being kind, helping me get away from Antonio... you're fair dinkum, girly." She put her arm around Tess to reciprocate. "I'm just trying to navigate my way through this strange new world. It's clear Amanda doesn't like me, and not many others here for that matter. So I'll just have to keep my head down and bum up. No fun, just focus on work."

Tess laughed. "Yeah, good luck with that, baby girl. I was watching you, and the guys hanging round, lookin' at you today. I kept having to ask Antonio to look straight ahead while I was working on him because he wouldn't stop turning his head to look over at you. Liam is obviously keen to get to know you better. The list goes on; it looked like bees around a honey pot today."

Charlotte stopped and gaped at Tess. "What? What... are you talking about? He... what?"

Tess laughed and continued walking, pulling Charlotte along in her stride. "Oh, lordy, you're *that* oblivious. It's okay, I'll watch out for you, girl. Just continue to be extra oblivious when Amanda's around, and we'll be alright."

Charlotte staggered onwards as they made their way out of the studio grounds towards a much-needed drink.

CHAPTER 6

Two months into the job, Charlotte felt the bone-weary tiredness that felt deeper than just physical fatigue. Although she'd had numerous jobs over the years, some of which she enjoyed and some she didn't, connection was something she craved. Most of her working life had been spent at the Gundagai pub, which certainly provided connection along with entertainment. Whilst the creative talents she innately possessed weren't utilised working behind a bar, there were a number of other benefits. Connections with her wonderful community were limitless, and Charlotte loved the philosophical conversations she'd often had with the locals. On her feet all day, she knew the pub managers loved her like a daughter and would support her no matter what. A true sense of belonging was something she found at that bar, and she keenly felt the absence of this in her new role.

Feeling like somebody cared, or that authentic, true connection with a person or people seemed to be increasingly unlikely in

Hollywood. Apart from the brief encounter with Antonio, Meeks' generosity at the cafe and Tess's sweet nature, real connection was sparse. Charlotte missed Mave's kindness, her wayward little brother, her mates. She missed Kev's big bear hugs, especially if she was having a rough day or had experienced some catastrophic mishap. Most of all, she missed honesty, and being able to call a spade a spade. Although she was a black sheep in this glittery town, Charlotte refused to change for these people, especially if she was only there for a year. *Stuff 'em...*

Prompted by her homesickness, Charlotte organised a video chat with Mave and Kev for the following Thursday evening, which would be Australia's Friday afternoon. Aware that phone reception would likely be bad and of her ex-employer's proclivity for hating technology, Charlotte braced herself for a brief, disrupted interaction.

"Shit... is this thing on? Mave, am I doing this right? Bloody phones..." boomed Kev's voice.

"Kev! Kev I can hear you! It's Charlotte, can you hear me?"

"Char! Where are you? I can hear ya, girl, just can't see ya! Where's that gorgeous mug of yours?"

"I'm here, matey, just press that thing that looks like a little camera, I reckon you've got video turned off."

Several slightly harsher swear words later, a close-up of Kev's nostril filled the screen temporarily before the picture blurred. Then two familiar faces materialised.

Charlotte felt her heart burst. "Oh my God, you guys... it's so good to see you. Far out, it seems like bloody years!"

"There's our girl!" Kev shouted. "Hey, half the town is here to say hi. Hang on, I'll turn this thing around. Hey everyone, it's Char!"

The screen spun round to reveal a packed-out pub behind him. A deafening roar emitted shortly before the noise-cancelling feature kicked in. Charlotte could just make out a sea of smiling faces and raised glasses. Tears pricked and her fingers instinctively moved to cover her lip as it started to quiver.

"Everyone misses the shit out of you, girl, so we're having a party in your honour."

The camera lingered on a man slumped over the bar, then the broad, smiling face of her younger brother filled the screen. Recognising Dylan, Charlotte didn't need to guess it was her father passed out next to him.

"Hey, big sis!" she heard him say as the image blurred, raising his glass and patting his father on the back, who stirred but didn't sit up. As the camera whirred back to the bar owners, Charlotte heard Dylan shouting something and the screen swung back to him.

"How you goin'? I'm back in town for the long weekend, the build-site is letting us have a decent break."

The phone wobbled and blurred again; Charlotte made out the words 'miss you Charlie' above the noise. Her little brother looked so grown-up.

"Yeah, call her yourself, ya camera hog!" Charlotte heard Kev shout off-screen. "You may be a big shot builder's apprentice now, but this is our bloody phone call!"

Mave said something, then her face appeared with her eyebrows furrowed.

"Have you lost weight? Char, are you eating over there? Why do you look tired? Looks like two crows have parked their arses under your eyes, girl, what's going on?"

Charlotte laughed and wiped her cheek.

"Just been a long day, darl. I'm eating, but food's a bit weird over here, nothing compared to Kev's gourmet fare, I'll tell you that for free! So, I see some things haven't changed eh; Dad's passed out as usual, and Dyl's home for the weekend. How are you guys doing, what's the goss?"

They nodded and looked at each other in contemplation before Kev answered in a loud whisper. "Well, one thing is we trialled a new bartender since you went and abandoned us, ya bastard. Some Norwegian backpacker. Lovely lass, just useless as tits on a bull. We'll give her another couple of weeks, then it might be sayonara spaghetti."

Sayonara spaghetti... one of Kev's favourite phrases. Charlotte laughed, despite feeling an unbidden stab of jealousy at the thought of some Scandinavian supermodel stealing her job.

"Aww, well they can't all be as good as me, Boss. I'm sure she'll find her feet soon enough."

"Oh, and speaking of my gourmet fare, we've decided to mix things up a bit, Char, as per your suggestion—bring some multicultural flair to good old Gundagai! We're doing different dinner themes during the week. Indian on Tuesdays, Italian on Wednesdays and something else... haven't quite decided... on Thursdays." Kev's face lit up with pride and excitement as he shared the news.

Charlotte gasped. "Holy shit, Kev, you told me to 'go get stuffed' when I suggested that idea!? So, all I had to do was leave, then you listen to me?"

Mave laughed, and Kev rolled his eyes.

"Yeah, whatever, shut ya face! Anyway, it's going off like a frog in a sock. The pub was packed on Tuesday, even though most of the dishes I made were vegetarian! We got rave reviews! Then Wednesday, we were turning people away. It was so packed. I made a few lasagnas, pizzas, spaghetti, shit loads of garlic bread and some homemade 'knocky'... no idea how to say the bloody thing but it tasted grouse."

Charlotte laughed, but more tears welled in her eyes. "It's g-n-o-c-c-h-i, Kev, –made from potatoes, the little seashell-type things? What did you mix it with, what kind of sauce?"

"Yeah, potato-something," Kev said dismissively. "I used a vegan recipe with roast pumpkin, pine nuts, spinach and some kinda weird plant-cheese shit."

Mave scratched Kev's beard lovingly. "So proud of him, darl, he's trying all sorts of new things, aren't you, Kev? Such a bloody good cook you are."

He smiled sheepishly and looked at his wife. "Thanks, Mavey. It's our Char that's given me a much-needed kick up the arse though. If our girl can up and leave Gundagai and work in a big scary place like Hollywood, I can try something new and cook foreign food."

"Good on you, Kev. You're a legend! Please hang onto those recipes so I can try them when I come home, especially the plant-cheese shit?"

After a brief delay where the screen froze, they both laughed.

"Sweetheart, I'll smother the bastard, don't you worry. Right, that's us eh, Mave? What about you, Char? What are they like over there, those Hollywood weirdos? You all booked in for a regular colonic and anal whitening yet?"

Charlotte barked with laughter. "Yeah, them and their bleached arses... oh, they're alright, I guess. It's just pretty phony. Like no one says how they really feel, or what they really think. People say what they think 'important' people want to hear, then judge everyone else behind their backs. They're all stunningly gorgeous on the outside... perfect teeth, and hair... and they eat like, nothing. When I go to eat a sandwich from the catering table, I get laughed at by all the skinny bitches for eating carbs."

"Streuth, Char! I wouldn't last five minutes over there, would I Mave?" Kev balked as Mave tutted and shook her head.

"We'd all stick out like dog's balls mate. I already do. I've made a dickhead out of myself so many times. The other day, I helped out this guy who looked like he was crying—really nice guy—turned out it was the bloody director of the movie we're working on." Charlotte slapped a hand over her face. "I was so embarrassed; I've been avoiding him ever since."

Mave responded first. "Why would you feel embarrassed about being nice to someone, love? It doesn't matter who he is; if he was upset and you were kind to him, what's so wrong about that?"

"Actually, yeah... that's a good point, Mave. That's how *we'd* do things. It doesn't matter what your title is, we don't give a shit about that stuff. Over here, people really do though. I guess I was more embarrassed because I hadn't done my homework. I didn't know this guy from a bar of soap."

Kev waved his hand dismissively. "Ahh, don't worry about it, darl. And don't let any of those snooty bleached arseholes get to you either. You're a beautiful soul and you shouldn't have to apologise for being bloody nice to someone. That's just dumb!"

Mave nodded enthusiastically and asked, "Who's this director guy anyway, would we know him? And is he a spunk?"

Charlotte laughed. "Well... yeah, he is easy on the eye. His name is Antonio Sanchez; he's acted in quite a few of his own movies, too. Action movies, but good quality, not boof-head, you know, ones that make you think a bit."

Kev and Mave nodded like they knew of him, although Charlotte strongly suspected they didn't.

"Is the work stuff good, Char, the make-up stuff?" asked Mave. "You said your boss is known for being a bit of a cow?"

Charlotte waited for the frozen screen to unfreeze before responding in case their run of excellent bandwidth luck had run out. In the meantime, she stifled the urge to laugh at the funny faces frozen on the screen. "Yeah, loving the actual work, it's really fun. I'm learning a lot! My boss—'Voss the Boss'—is pretty scary, but I'm just avoiding her as much as I can."

"We're so prou—" The screen froze again with Kev baring his crooked teeth in mid-speech.

Charlotte waited, then said, "Can you hear me guys?"

A minute went by, but still Kev's last words hung in the air, his agape mouth still displayed on the screen. Charlotte's phone dinged with a message:

Sorry, darl, bloody internet shit itself again. We love you, we're so proud of you. Have the best adventures, we're all gunning for you, Char. We'll all be here waiting right here for you when you're ready to come home with plant-cheese shit, Kev & Mave xx

Charlotte re-read the text message several times. Tears ran down her cheeks. How cruelly she missed them, and that sweet ache of homesickness squirmed in the pit of her stomach once again.

Some things would change, and some would be frozen in time. Charlotte snorted as she remembered her father's parting words to her: "Two months sober, Charlie. I'm getting my shit together now."

Sure you are, Dad.

Charlotte rolled her eyes, remembering all the failed promises that came before that one. Her mind leafed through the next tid-bit from the phone call—her little brother.

She felt a swell of pride, remembering the pains she went through to get him that tradie apprenticeship and going out on a limb for him. Knowing the builder was reputable as well as a decent bloke, Charlotte had hoped rather than believed Dylan would commit to being a good trainee. She knew she had to intervene and break the well-worn pattern of alcoholism in their family, or her beloved brother would be next to throw his life down the toilet. Charlotte had done her best to parent him in the absence of any decent pillar of authority and felt getting him onto a building site or off to the mines would be his best chance. She couldn't look after him forever, as Mave and Kev constantly reminded her. She needed to live her own life. Which was why she was here.

Charlotte came back to the room after being lost in thought for some time. She glanced at the clock through watery eyes and realised she needed to get to bed; it was just shy of midnight. She knew she'd need her sleep tonight as tomorrow was an early start, working solo with her boss on-site. She felt a looming dread and figured avoidance wouldn't be a viable option.

How can I be true to myself without getting into trouble?

CHAPTER 7

Charlotte's phone alarm buzzed, waking her from a deep sleep. She'd been dreaming she was back in the bar in Gundagai, enjoying time with the gang. What puzzled her as she sat up and wiped the drool from her mouth was the presence of Antonio and two little girls, who appeared to be his daughters. They were all having such fun, eating, drinking, laughing and meeting all of her family and friends. Antonio was praising Kev about how good his gnocchi was. The dream was so vivid, so real. What was more, Antonio and Charlotte were *together*. That feeling of being in love and having her own family washed over her as she drank water from the bottle beside her bed.

Okay, that was weird.

Glancing at her phone still sitting on a milk crate next to her bed, she realised she could easily find out the answer. Did Antonio have two daughters? *It wouldn't matter if he did because it was just a dream and that would never happen in a million years. You are here to work, Charlotte, not fall in love or date anyone from work... let alone the bloody director. Now, snap out of it!*

Charlotte took a deep breath, got up, opened the curtains and looked out at the dark skyline, with building lights twinkling in the smoggy pink haze.

Arriving early at the studio's designated shuttle stop, Charlotte darted into the building to grab what was needed for the day. She had been advised yesterday that all necessary materials would be waiting in a pile for her to load onto the shuttle bus. Amanda would meet her on site, preferring her own means of transport. The rest of the small team were in a mandatory training session that couldn't be rescheduled. Amanda had told them this with a set jaw and her usual smiling-yet-furious delivery, the sickly-sweet voice betraying the message.

If she hates us, and all of this so much, why is she doing it? Could I ever ask her, or would that be poking the bear?

"Good morning!" Charlotte said cheerily to the driver as he got out to load the make-up suitcases and various containers she'd brought out.

"Uh, good... good morning, Miss," he said, slightly startled.

"Can I help you with those? Some of them are kinda heavy."

The driver, roughly in his mid-forties, looked perplexed. "No... no it's okay, thank you, Miss. I'll look after this. Please, get in and have a seat; we'll be departing shortly for Forest Park."

"All good, thanks, matey!" She gave him two thumbs up and climbed into the small bus.

Another one for the 'freaked out' list...

Charlotte took a seat a few rows back from the driver. The sun was rising, and more people were out and about; she saw Gus open the little boom-gate shed and smiled to herself. *He's such a sweetheart...*

As she sat and watched various studio crew members arriving, her dream continued to pick at the back of her mind.

Screw it...

Taking out her phone from her jacket pocket, she typed Antonio's name into the search bar. Articles appeared describing a messy divorce and both being seen out in public with other potential partners. His estranged wife, Lucia, was claiming Antonio cheated on her and, according to one sensationalist tabloid, was aiming to 'clean out his bank account and ruin his career.' The article also suggested she wanted sole custody of their kids.

Oh my God...

In one of the pictures were two adorable little girls. Exactly as she'd dreamed, both holding hands with their parents. A shiver descended Charlotte's spine.

I must have seen that picture somewhere before... doesn't mean anything.

With a jump, the bus's front door shut, and the engine started. Placing her phone down on the soft seat next to her, Charlotte tapped her cheeks and made herself comfortable. She gazed through the windows as they made their way past the entrance, out of the studio grounds that Charlotte had been told would soon be turned into a carpark. She had never cared much since she didn't own a car and would never drive anywhere anyway.

As they headed out into the morning traffic, the driver craned his neck to face Charlotte. "We've just got one more pick-up, then we'll be on our way, Miss. Should be on site in around forty-five minutes."

Charlotte peered over the top of the seats as she listened. "No worries, thank you!"

As they made their way through the streets of downtown Hollywood, Charlotte watched daily life in motion outside the window. Little dogs dressed in outfits matching their owners, people on their phones, businesses promising encounters with celebrities. Famous landmarks she'd only seen in movies passed by, now becoming commonplace. She smiled as she thought of Sheridan Street in Gundagai and the stark contrasts between the two locales. Homelessness wasn't really an issue back home, since if anyone had a problem, they'd be looked after by the small community. On a number of occasions, Mave and Kev had allowed people to stay upstairs in the pub's hotel rooms free of charge if they were going through a rough patch. Here, the homeless were stepped over if they took up too much room on the sidewalk. Charlotte supposed it wasn't just Hollywood; having travelled little during her young life, she didn't have much to compare to. Sydney was loud, chaotic and way too fast for her liking but at least she understood the underlying culture.

The shuttle turned into the gates of another studio and Charlotte saw a handful of people waiting out the front of a fancy glass building with the logo emblazoned across the front. She recognised a few faces from one of the off-site sets they were working on, and it prompted a vague memory. Charlotte had found herself so busy and her focus solely on her work that she often ignored the environments around her. More than once, she'd found a colleague yelling or tapping her on the arm to break her reverie, blissfully unaware of what was happening around her.

As the group boarded the bus, the first person sneered when he saw Charlotte. Turning to the friend behind him, Charlotte distinctly heard the words, "Forest Gump." Her smile that greeted them morphed into a grimace as they walked past her, sniggering to themselves. *So that nickname is catching on... cool.* Sighing heavily, she looked out the window again.

"Ahh, we meet again, young lady! Is this seat taken?"

Charlotte looked up to see a familiar face. "Meeks! You beauty! Of course, please, sit down!" She quickly moved her phone and bag.

He smiled broadly at her, then looked to the back of the bus. "Hey, you three, have you met Charlotte? She's one of the most promising young make-up artists in Hollywood. You'd do well to treat her with respect."

Charlotte heard muttering, then a couple of half-hearted *hellos*. She turned in her seat and bellowed "hello" enthusiastically, prompting a chuckle from Meeks.

"So, how have you been? No call from you. Did you throw my number away or something?"

Charlotte laughed. "No! God no. I've just been trying to find my feet, matey.... Saints alive, it's been busy. The hours are crazy! I just get home and collapse. I've been very boring indeed. How are you? What's the goss?"

"What's the *goss*," he pondered. "Well, we've managed to get funding for a movie trilogy, which is pretty cool. So, production will start soon."

"Was that your studio? I mean the one you're based at? Or are you the boss man? I'm still getting my head around who and what is where."

"It's okay, there's a lot to learn. Yeah, I guess you could say it's my studio." He looked like he was bracing for follow up questions.

"That's cool! So, what restaurants have you been to lately? Any food porn to share with your old mate Forrest Gump?" She elbowed Meeks in the ribs, prompting him to throw back his head with laughter.

"Ahh, Charlotte, you are such a breath of much-needed fresh air. Uh... what have I had... well, we went to a Korean BBQ place on the weekend. That was cool. And a very good but very expensive sushi bar. Do you like Asian food?"

"I LOVE Asian food. I tried sushi for the second time the other night, not on purpose really; it was the only place open. I reckon that stuff was laced with crack though. I can't stop thinking about it."

Meeks continued to laugh.

"So, what's your movie trilogy about?" she asked, cocking her head. "Is it about sushi?"

"I don't know if I *can* go to dinner with you, Charlotte. I'd be laughing too hard to eat anything." He wiped his eyes with the back of his hand. "No, unfortunately for us, it's not about sushi. It's a post-apocalyptic sci-fi, wasteland, survival of the fittest... that kind of thing. Disaster movies are hot right now. Big budget, big names, big guns, everything. Just big."

Charlotte's eyes widened. "That sounds awesome! The location we're going to sounds just like that; oh wait, is that why you're going?"

Meeks nodded. "Yeah, we're doing a bit of pre-location scouting. Myself and those bone-heads back there who work for me. And also checking out the talent... I'm meeting with your boss this morning." He winked, and a mischievous look spread across his face.

"Ahh, I see," she said knowingly, a feeling of slight panic fluttering in her stomach. "Well, I'll try and be on my best behaviour and not say or do anything idiotic. Can't make any promises though. I make a dickhead out of myself on a regular basis."

They chatted the entire way as the view outside changed from the bustling city to a barren, desert-like landscape. Before long, the bus slowed and turned off the freeway into a smaller road that wound through scrubby brown fields and the occasional shack. Dust plumes spewed from the back of the bus when the road changed from paved to gravel, and it grew bumpy as the surface became more rutted. Charlotte had been enjoying her conversation with Meeks so much that she'd temporarily forgotten where they were going or what she was going to do next. They slowed further and turned at a flag marker towards what looked like a campsite. As the bus came to a stop, Charlotte noted the crew setting up and spotted a few familiar faces. One in particular sprang out of the crowd.

"Ahh, there she is, matey, 'Voss the Boss.' Oh... and she doesn't look happy. Surprise, surprise. This should be an interesting day!"

Meeks moved his head for a clearer view of the woman as Charlotte saw the bus driver open the door and make his way outside.

"Jesus, you're right... it literally looks like there's a storm cloud over her head," Meeks muttered.

"Must be tough for a woman in this business though, after all these years. Amanda's been running things for a long time, so I guess she must be doing something right."

They sat quietly as they witnessed Amanda gesturing wildly while talking on her phone. Her face contorted angrily as she ended the call and, if looks could kill, the device in her hand would end up melting. She then directed her anger at the driver, now popping open the storage containers under the bus. Charlotte and Meeks looked at each other from the safety of inside the shuttle, grimaced, then started chuckling.

"Shit, mate, we better strap our nuts on for this," Charlotte uttered, prompting more laughter from Meeks. They sat and waited as the bus emptied, watching Amanda continue to berate the shuttle driver. In an instant, she changed her expression, and when Charlotte craned her neck to see who or what had prompted this transformation, she saw Antonio.

Oh, crapping crapsicles.

She'd managed to avoid him successfully since their first meeting, but with such a small crew out there today, avoidance was not really an option.

Meeks turned to Charlotte as he stood. "What is it, kiddo, you okay? Did I miss Amanda disembowelling someone?"

"Nah… I just saw that the director is here," Charlotte whispered as Meeks stood aside, allowing her to walk ahead of him.

She smiled in appreciation.

"Antonio Sanchez? Oh, that's great! I wasn't one hundred percent sure if he'd be here today. Now there's a nice guy."

Charlotte's heart thumped wildly.

Exiting the bus and stepping onto the dusty ground, she felt a warm breeze on her face and the smell of the arid desert, calming her hammering heart. Charlotte followed Meeks to where Amanda, Antonio and a few 'puffer-jacket' crew members with clipboards were congregating. There, standing back a few paces behind Antonio, was the little hamster-guy Charlotte had seen at the coffee shop so many weeks ago. He still looked just as terrified.

Amanda and Antonio looked over as they approached, with Charlotte lagging behind Meeks. She watched the director's face light up when he saw Meeks, and the two greeted each other warmly. Antonio looked to Meek's side briefly and did a double take; his eyes locked with Charlotte's. She felt her knees weaken. His eyes... those beautiful, chocolate-brown eyes... and that hair falling across his tanned brow. After what could have been an eternity, Charlotte snapped out of her stupor and tucked her hair behind her ear nervously as she looked at the ground. She felt Meeks take her hand gently.

"Hey, Ant, I've just had the *best* bus ride with one of your special-effects make-up artists. Charlotte Grant, a smart, funny and beautiful Australian girl having to put up with us American morons."

The group laughed, and Charlotte could feel herself blushing as all eyes swung upon her; she looked up to see Antonio staring and Amanda glaring.

"Charlotte, you're finally here! Just looking at the equipment you brought—uh, did I make a huge mistake in hiring you?" She tried to say it in a sweet, joking way, giving a little chuckle, but Charlotte furrowed her brow, sensing the spitefulness, and glanced around the confused-looking group before Meeks squeezed her hand.

"Hello, Amanda? I'm Edward Meeks, nice to meet you," he said with practiced charm. "I've heard so much about you. Charlotte and I took the scheduled shuttle bus together; are we both late?"

Amanda smiled as she shook his outstretched hand. Choosing to ignore his comment, she directed her dagger-eyes back at Charlotte. "You've forgotten to bring two packs of prosthetics.

Were my instructions not clear enough for you, sweetheart? Now I'm going to have to pay for a courier to bring them because of your stupidity." Her sweet-sounding voice was discordant with her angry words and facial expression.

Antonio looked quizzically at Amanda, then at Meeks. "I'm sure it was just a misunderstanding, Amanda, have you never made a mistake?" He looked back at Charlotte and smiled. "I've been trying to speak with you, Charlotte. I think you've been avoiding me... I still owe you a coffee."

Oh crap... crap! Of all the things I wish you hadn't mentioned right now in front of everyone, completely out of context...

Amanda's head snapped back to Antonio, then towards Charlotte, who was smiling awkwardly, trying desperately to will invisibility. Amanda opened her mouth to speak, but Meeks intervened.

"Hey, Ant, speaking of coffee, can I please get some? We should probably leave these ladies to get set up. Amanda, pleasure to meet you. We're still on for 10am? And you, m'lady, thank you for your wonderful company. I'm looking forward to seeing your brilliance in action today." He gave a little bow for Charlotte.

Antonio beamed at Charlotte as Meeks ushered them towards a marquee, presumably the catering tent. She took a deep breath as Amanda's eyes fixed on hers and stepped towards her like a wind up toy about to explode.

Charlotte held up her hand in anticipation of Amanda's fury. "Amanda, before you say anything, I just picked up the equipment left in the designated spot. I have the text message to prove it. I just followed the instructions I was given. I'm happy to cover the cost of the courier if I've acted in error. Could I please just start setting up?"

This seemed to take the wind out of Amanda's sails, and she paused, looking at Charlotte as if calculating her response.

"I *will* take it out of your pay cheque as a lesson never to trust other people. You should have checked the equipment list, that's a no-brainer. And what the *hell* was that about buying the *director* a coffee?"

Charlotte smiled sweetly and took a deep breath. "It's a long story, and I didn't buy him anything. It's a total misunderstanding. Can we get set up? We've got a big day and I'm really keen to get started."

Amanda narrowed her eyes, her stern gaze boring into Charlotte's skull. They held eye contact for what seemed poised to become an intense standoff, with Charlotte determined to stand her ground.

"Remember the rules, Charlotte. If I find out you're trying to get in anyone's pants, *especially* Antonio's, you'll wish you'd never been born. Now, take this stuff to that tent over there; that's where you'll be working. No breaks until 1pm. Now get to work!" She turned and stomped off towards the catering tent.

Charlotte's insides squirmed as she watched Amanda's departure, her thoughts consumed by the hellishly awkward encounter.

Antonio... oh my God, he's handsome.... Was he looking at me in 'that' way...? No. Maybe? He's so nice... he was sticking up for me when that troll was attacking.... Okay, Grant, get your shit together! Shake it off, it's game-time!

Turning on her heel, she headed to the make-up tent. She had the feeling today was indeed going to prove a challenging day.

CHAPTER 8

Charlotte ran her hands through her ponytail and felt the dust collect between her fingers. She'd stepped out of the make-up tent for a moment for some fresh air and to bask in the last of the Californian sun sinking behind the desert in a blaze of orange and pink. It had been another long day of filming, and the last of the cleaning and packing up had finished. With a few spare minutes until the shuttle departed back to the studio grounds and the management team gone, Charlotte had a quiet moment to mentally unpack the wild events from earlier that day.

Meeks had been her saviour, and she doubted whether she'd still be standing had it not been for his support. Although Amanda had begrudgingly granted her a ten-minute break for lunch, reasoning that Charlotte was the only make-up artist on site, her brief respite had been cut even shorter, to the point there'd hardly been a break at all. If she wanted to complain about it, there were unions that would advocate for better working conditions, but that would not help her career in the long run, so she had to accept it as part of the job. But at what cost? Meeks had brought her coffee and little snacks, always with a gentle pat on the back and words of encouragement, and during the lunchtime hour, he had delivered a plate filled with little sandwiches to the make-up tent.

"Oh, matey... you are just the best. You're spoiling me rotten!" Charlotte gushed as he wordlessly handed over her refilled water bottle. He then stood back and admired the work she was doing on the actor sitting in her make-up chair.

"Charlotte, your work is... incredible. Do you mind if I look closer?"

Charlotte and the actor in question nodded in agreement in perfect synchrony, as if their heads were both operated by a single brain.

"Go for your life! I reckon this warrior is finished now anyway." Charlotte used the interlude to gulp down water from her now full bottle. The conditions out there were so dry, and as Charlotte smiled, it felt like her cheeks were covered in scales.

"Incredible... the detail in these wounds." He bent over, peering closely at the actor's face. "What's this pus stuff?"

"It's like a type of gel, it's really cool. If you add bits of like... grit or something over the top of the ooze, it looks even more realistic I find." Charlotte rubbed her fingers together descriptively, then continued to drink water to relieve her parched throat.

"Wow... I'd... you can't even tell it's fake. And that's not even looking through a camera. Girl, I've never seen work like this." Meeks stepped back and put his hands on his hips. "You're... you're truly amazing!"

"Aww, thank you," she said with a smile and a slight blush.

"I'll be back shortly," said the actor as he climbed out of the chair and walked out of the tent.

Meeks and Charlotte followed the actor outside into the bright afternoon sunshine.

Meeks turned to look at Charlotte. "Honey, we really need to talk. The way you're being treated is... well, it's not acceptable. It's obvious you're gifted, but you're being treated like garbage. People are noticing, and they're talking. A few of us are going to the bar around the corner from the studio tonight, can you please join us there? There are some people I really want you to meet, and who really want to talk to you. Amanda won't be there; she won't even know about it, so it's totally safe." He held up his hand as if anticipating an objection.

Still, Charlotte paused to consider the offer. "I dunno... I just don't want to ruffle any feathers, matey. If I cause trouble, it's sayonara spaghetti for me. My working visa could be revoked and maybe I'll never be able to come back. There's a lot riding on this. I'm sure Amanda is just under heaps of stress; she's running her own business in this male-dominant industry, you know... maybe it's just a rough patch or something?"

Meeks dropped his chin but kept his eyes locked with Charlotte's. "Char, the woman is pure ev- wait... 'Sayonara spaghetti?'" Meeks chuckled and cocked his head. "Look, kid, there are ways around these things. Antonio and I have been talking about you... he's asked *a lot* of questions... he's obviously completely smitten with you. Will you at least please come for one drink?"

Charlotte straightened, as if about to spring into action.

"*What?* What do you mean he—"

From nowhere, Amanda appeared in front of the tent, her expression unreadable. Still gripping her bottle, Charlotte quickly took another swig of water to prevent her from speaking first. *Shit, did she just hear our conversation? Shit!*

"Edward, can we get your opinion on something please? Charlotte... they're... happy with what you're producing today. The crew said they're... getting some good shots." Amanda delivered robotically, apparently struggling to impart the positive feedback. Glancing briefly back at Meeks, she turned and hurried off.

Charlotte's eyes widened as she swallowed her mouthful of water, dumbstruck by what had just unfolded.

Meeks squawked with laughter. "What the *hell* was that? Was that a compliment? From *Amanda Voss*? Woooow!"

"I know," said Charlotte.

"Okay, I gotta do this thing, then I need to split. Bar, tonight, okay? I have your number now, don't make me come after you, girl."

"I shouldn't have sent you that stupid kitten meme during the bus ride, cos you'd have no idea what my number was." Charlotte sighed. "Alright, I'll come. Fair warning, I'll look like I've been dragged through a bush backwards... and can't promise I'll be able to string a coherent sentence together."

"You're gorgeous just the way you are. I'll see you later, kid." With that, he turned and walked out of the tent, pointing back at her as he exited.

Antonio... might be a little smitten....? Oh my God... oh MY GOD!

Before she could process those words, another group of actors arrived in need of her expertise, so she got back to it.

Snapping out of her trance, Charlotte came back to the moment, staring at the stunning sunset that bathed her face in warm light. She now found herself pondering whether she should just go home, back to Australia. Gundagai would probably feel too small for her now, having been in such a big place, but she felt certain there'd be job opportunities in Sydney. This was all so much, and if people were indeed talking, then trouble was undoubtedly brewing.

In essence, joining Meeks and the crew for a quick drink and a chat was no big deal, and before long she would be collapsing on her tiny bed in her shoebox apartment. But Charlotte's intuition told her this decision held much bigger implications. By joining them, she'd be walking down the path that might start an irreversible chain reaction of events. A shiver ran down her spine, and she rubbed her tired goose-bumped arms.

Charlotte felt that same warm desert breeze carrying an earthy grass smell caress her face and closed her eyes to fully drink it in. William's words about hearing the pulse of the earth came back to her, and she instantly felt the connection to the land. Taking a deep breath, she opened her eyes. Two large birds were lazily circling way up in the sky. Were they eagles? Or vultures?

Suddenly, one of them dropped, diving straight towards her, closely followed by the other. Charlotte blanched and took a step backwards, preparing herself to run. Hurtling towards the ground, the birds pulled up just short before touching down a few yards away; dust plumes rose as their massive wings flapped. Charlotte saw a brown, furry blur disappear behind a clump of grass, and suspected their intended target had narrowly escaped a grisly fate.

The eagles fluttered their huge and majestic wings and looked at Charlotte, completely nonplussed. A loud clatter from behind made them all glance nervously, shaking Charlotte from her reverie and scaring the birds away.

Having visited the bar months ago on a Friday after work, Charlotte found the current Wednesday night crowd much quieter. Despite a hasty make-up application, hair fix and change of shirt before leaving the site, Charlotte still felt tired and self-conscious among the groups of people dotted around the venue as she stepped inside. Their designer clothes hung effortlessly off their flawless, sculpted bodies with sparkling jewellery shining from the subdued lighting. Lo-fi house music played softly in the background and a pleasant chatter and laughter met her ears. It smelled like expensive perfume and oak wood rather than the beer-soaked carpet and body odour smells she was accustomed to in the Gundagai pub.

Charlotte made her way towards the bar and glimpsed Meeks and a handful of other people she didn't recognise to his left. His face beamed when he saw Charlotte, patted the person he was talking to on the shoulder and made his way over to her.

"Charlotte, my darling, I'm so happy you're here!" He kissed her on the cheek. "Let me get you a drink. What's your poison?"

"Uh... I'll just have a beer thanks, matey! A Budweiser on tap would be awesome."

"You got it!" he responded before ordering with the bar staff, asking them to put it on the tab. As the barman grabbed a glass and started pouring, Meeks stood behind Charlotte and gently massaged her shoulders. She groaned appreciatively, and didn't notice when a man approached because she had partly closed her eyes.

"So, this is the girl my husband can't stop talking about," said a kind voice. Charlotte opened her eyes to see a tanned, beautifully groomed man with silver-grey hair, slightly taller than herself. Charlotte gasped and shot out her hand.

"Oh my gosh, hello! Meeks, you sly fox, I didn't know you were married! I'm Charlotte!"

"I see what you mean, Edward," he said, his blue eyes staring mischievously as he took Charlotte's hand. "I'm James, it's lovely to meet you in person, my dear. I've heard so much about you."

Charlotte grimaced. "Shit, I hope it was all good. I can be a bloody galah sometimes." She reached for the icy cold beer and took a long sip, watching the two men laugh. "Ahh, beer. The cause of and solution to all of life's problems," she said with a sigh, her shoulders dropping.

James nodded knowingly and pointed at her. "Excellent *Simpson's* reference there—great writers—I like this one!" On that, he excused himself.

Charlotte smiled and watched him walk towards the bathroom, then turned back to Meeks now leaning on the bar.

"Dude, your hubby is such a spunk! What a gorgeous couple you are. It's no surprise you're off the market."

Meeks feigned embarrassment. "Ahh, he's okay," he said, waving dismissively. "Anyway, okay, Char, it's business time. Here's the situation: apart from my company that wants to steal you, we've got two other picture company heads here. We've been talking about how that troll Amanda doesn't deserve you. The way you handle yourself so smoothly and with such professionalism is to be commended. Amanda can break—and has broken, believe me, I've seen it—the strongest of us."

Charlotte listened and continued to sip her beer, enjoying the refreshment on her parched throat.

Meeks went on. "What salary are you after? And what kind of movies do you want to work on? I know you said you like working on the gory prosthetics stuff. We can make it happen; you just have to say the word."

"I... um... salary? I... don't know. I guess more than what I'm on now, just so I can rent a nicer apartment and save a bit... maybe? Shit, mate, I hadn't really thought about it... I was just trying to get through the first six months without screwing it up. I really didn't expect I'd have any other choices, what with my visa and all that shemozzle."

Meeks leaned forward and squeezed her arm. "Honey, people with talent and who are lovely and easy to work with always have more choices. Luck is always a factor, along with who you know, but it's also about what you can offer. You're rare, Charlotte; you're sweet, and honest and—damn girl—you're amazing at what you do. No one can believe Amanda is treating you this way, considering the jewel she has in her hands."

Charlotte stared blankly at him. A little gas rose in her throat and resonated as a cute burp; her hand flew to her mouth to cover it but was a microsecond too slow.

Meeks noticed and stifled a laugh, shaking his head. "So, that's your response? You're just going to burp at me?" he asked with a straight face.

Charlotte, her hand still over her mouth, started laughing uncontrollably.

"I can see why you'd want me around, mate," she said, taking another sip of beer. "I've got class coming out of my arse." Realising her top lip was covered in beer foam, she wiped it off with the back of her hand.

Meeks laughed, shook his head again and looked at her adoringly.

"I realise this is a lot to lay on you, especially after such a big day. Please just promise me you'll think about it, okay? It's really difficult for me to stand by and watch you getting treated like crap. I'm kinda fond of you, kid, and I want to help you out."

"Aww, Meeksy, you're such a ledge, thank you, and—"

Charlotte's eyes darted to her left at the man who had appeared from nowhere—Antonio. As if under some kind of trance, she melted into those eyes again, unaware of anything else. She couldn't look away. She felt a hand on the small of her back and snapped out of whatever spell he'd put her under, feeling weak in the knees.

"Char—CHAR? James is wondering if you want to play a game of pool with us, doubles? Liam wants to be your partner." Meeks pointed over to a waving Liam holding two pool cues.

Charlotte blinked rapidly and smiled at him, waving the wrong hand and spilling beer down the front of her shirt.

Of the two men, Antonio sprang into action first. "Oh no, let me help you with that, Miss." He turned to the bar staff. "Could we get a towel please, we've had a little accident."

The server smiled nervously and at once handed Antonio a towel.

He took it gratefully and applied it to Charlotte's chest before suddenly realising what he was doing.

"My goodness... oh, Charlotte, I'm so sorry. Please, you, um... you can obviously do that yourself." His eyes darted, trying to avoid looking directly at Charlotte's chest.

"Ahem, well it looks like Antonio's looking after you... I'm, uh, gonna go and stand over there now... Char, come over when you're ready, honey." Meeks winked and patted both their shoulders playfully.

Charlotte looked up red faced and nodded. "Cool, cool, cool... thanks, yeah. Antonio, thank you, gosh, I'm such a clutz. I was definitely born with the goofball gene." She dabbed her chest and attempted normal dialogue, flicking her hair out of her face.

Antonio laughed nervously, then leaned awkwardly on the bar.

It seemed to Charlotte that he couldn't decide what to do with his arms and hands, like he had one too many. Then he jumped, as if thinking of something groundbreaking.

"Let me get you another drink! Miss, excuse me, could we get another one of what this young lady was drinking please, thank you."

Once more, the server obliged without hesitation, and Charlotte could see her hands shaking slightly as she poured the beer.

She's nervous... Antony is a really, really big deal... and he's trying not to stare at my beer-stained boobs...

Charlotte finished drying her chest, put the damp towel on the bar and smiled gratefully at the server. Realising the ridiculous nature of the situation, she looked at her feet and then up at Antonio's face... and started to laugh. At first, he looked quizzical, but he soon joined in with a relaxed and relieved laugh.

The server placed the beer in front of Charlotte on the bar and nodded. As she took the glass with both hands, she glanced at Antonio's t-shirt and did a double-take—it was a grainy depiction of two eagles, just like the ones she'd seen earlier.

"Thanks so much, Antonio, I really appreciate it," Charlotte said as grabbed the beer on the bar.

"My pleasure, it's the least I can do, Charlotte," he said with a smile. "I owed you a drink anyway."

Charlotte suddenly became very aware of her weakened knees, feeling they could give at any moment. *God, he smells amazing...*

Antonio cleared his throat and suddenly looked serious. "Hey, um, has Meeks spoken to you? We've been discussing you a great deal today. It must be hard moving from another country into this crazy American culture and this bizarre industry. I remember when I moved back from Spain; it was a huge adjustment, but at least my family has been here for a long time."

"Oh, okay, when did you move back? I can imagine it's pretty different from Spain. It's certainly different from Gundagai." She chuckled, eager to learn more about Antonio and avoid going over the conversation she'd had with Meeks.

"It feels like a lifetime ago, but I think about fifteen years or so? I moved back with my wife... ex-wife now, and we had our baby girls here. I've been making movies since before I left Spain though. Huge learning curve there."

Charlotte desperately wanted to ask more probing questions but was aware this might not be the place.

He continued before she could comment. "Uh, Charlotte, I also wanted to ask you... and you're totally okay to say no, please don't feel obligated. I was just uh... thinking you'd be new to our theme parks and stuff. Have you—uh, have you been to Disneyland yet?"

Charlotte gasped. "No! I haven't! I've always wanted to go. I've heard they've opened a couple of new rides! Work has been so busy; I haven't had the chance to think about it. I mean, and that's fine, like, I'm so grateful to be working and it's great, I'm really grateful; work's awesome."

Stop talking Charlotte.

Antonio didn't seem to notice Charlotte's babbling and suddenly seemed very interested in his feet. "I was, uh, well, I'm taking my girls this weekend when I have them, and I uh... would you like to—"

"Hey, what's taking so long, Aussie girl—are we playing pool or what?" Liam asked as he approached them. Antonio's face fell and he looked resignedly at the film star.

"Hello, Liam," Antonio said flatly.

Liam gave the director an acknowledging nod. "Hey, Mr Sanchez, how's it hangin'?" Liam smiled cheekily while passing a pool cue to Charlotte. "Come on, we need to show these guys how it's done!" Liam slid his hand around Charlotte's waist and pulled her towards him.

Her eyes widened at this overly familiar gesture and looked at Antonio, now glaring at Liam.

Hello ground. Can you please open up and swallow me. Thanks.

Charlotte smiled apologetically, just managing to grab her beer and thank Antonio as she was swept away by the film star. As the foursome talked about the pool rules and decided on who was first, Charlotte looked back to the bar and saw a small, olive-skinned woman approach Antonio. Manicured hands flailing above her tiny frame, she pointed in Charlotte's direction as her voice elevated, making Antonio look even more miserable. Charlotte couldn't make out what she was saying. He threw up his hands and walked towards the exit; the small woman's loud, screechy voice followed him as he departed. As she tottered after Antonio on her impossibly high heels, she turned and looked at Charlotte, arms set straight at her sides, eyes narrowed.

That must be Lucia... blimey... dynamite comes in small packages...

Following the couple with her eyes, Charlotte's attention was again snapped as she felt a tapping on her shoulder. Bringing her head back to her surroundings, she was startled when a broad-faced man suddenly appeared in front of her.

"Char, honey, I want you to meet Brian, my colleague over at Universal—Brian, this is Charlotte, the amazingly talented new make-up artist from Australia. She's currently working for Amanda Voss." Meek's introduction dripped with disdain as he mentioned Amanda.

Brian smiled kindly, then winced comically. "Hello there, Charlotte, welcome to Hollywood! Meeks has been raving about you. It's great to meet you in person! What do you think of our little town so far?"

Charlotte gave the biggest smile she could muster, given the confusing last few minutes. "Hey, Brian, nice to meet you, mate! Yeah, Hollywood is grouse, like really amazing, but pretty different to what I'm used to. There are only two thousand people in the whole of Gundagai, so yeah, it's a little different!" She shook Brian's hand cheerfully.

"Haha, I bet! Meeks said you like special effects, the blood and gore stuff, rather than the glamour make-up work?"

Charlotte nodded enthusiastically as she sipped her beer. "Yeah, that's right! I'm definitely not a girly-girl, as you can probably tell, so the guts and eyeballs stuff are definitely my cup of tea... so to speak."

"Ahh, excellent. I'm exactly the same. My wife is the opposite. She can't stand the gore, but I love it—we've got a big horror movie franchise coming up soon, and we desperately need artists like you."

He watched eagerly for Charlotte's reaction.

Hells bells, what is this? I feel like I'm first prize in a bloody meat tray raffle...

Thankfully, before Charlotte could respond, yet another tap on her arm by Liam prompting her to play saved her from saying anything without time to actually consider it. She apologised and graciously accepted Brian's card as he made his way over to the bar, promising her they would talk again soon.

"Girl, you've got some big-name execs eating out of the palm of your hand tonight. You've got a director drooling over you." Liam leaned forward and whispered, "How are they going to respond when you go out to dinner with a big movie star tomorrow night?"

Charlotte looked at him, dumbstruck.

"What's your favourite cuisine, Aussie girl?"

"Uh... I dunno. I eat pretty much anything... why? What's going on?"

"What's your vibe?"

Charlotte stared at him with a cocked eyebrow.

"Vibe, you know–what are you into?"

"Huh?"

"Never mind. I'll pick you up at eight."

Charlotte snorted, holding her pool cue and blinking rapidly. "Uh... what? I... Huh? Dude! I can't go out to dinner with you! My boss will fire me!"

Liam shook his head. "Nah, she'll never find out. The place I want to take you is pretty exclusive, no paps."

Paps?

Charlotte continued to search for an appropriate response as Liam calmly took his turn, sinking a striped, yellow ball. Meeks and his husband were smiling mischievously from across the pool table as she stood with her mouth open.

"Uh... I... don't think..."

Liam walked up to her, prowling like a cat. His scent played in her nostrils, and Charlotte's head spun with his energy and confidence.

"Honey, this is happening. No one will find out; you're not going to get fired. It's okay. Trust me!" He flattened some stray hairs on her head and stroked her jawline. Charlotte found herself overpowered, smiling and laughing goofily.

"Okay. Okay, Liam Reeves, I'll go on a date with you."

CHAPTER 9

Since Charlotte arrived in Hollywood, it rained for the first time. Not just showers but a consistent downpour. It was seemingly all anyone talked about. Rain was considered a blessing back home in Australia, so she didn't mind the 30-minute walk from her apartment to the studio, using a large Gundagai-branded tourism umbrella she'd found tucked away in one of her bags.

Mave. Still looking after me, a million miles away.

Resisting the temptation to splash in the puddles for the majority of her walk, Charlotte finally indulged and jumped into one, laughing with joy as she kicked at the deep water. A thong flew off her foot and landed in a puddle in front of an approaching couple. She smiled when they looked at her quizzically and rounded the floating thong.

Geez, lighten up you two, it's only water.

Balancing on one leg with her foot submerged, she became

aware of a large, black limousine slowing beside her. The windows were glazed, so as it pulled up all she could see was her confused expression in the reflection. As the window slid down, she made out a familiar face in the darkened interior.

"Hello Charlotte!" said Antonio. "We are just on the way to the studio. Can we offer you a ride?"

Charlotte became aware of how ridiculous she looked.

"Oh... hey, Antonio! Uh... sure, okay... I am saturated though. I don't want to mess up your lovely car."

"Not to worry, Charlotte, a few in here have also been jumping in puddles," he said with a cheeky grin.

A second later, the driver's door opened and a very tall man with a dark complexion climbed effortlessly out of the car and opened the passenger door for Charlotte.

"Oh, matey, it's okay, you don't have to do that! I don't want you to get drenched, too!" Charlotte unfurled her umbrella and pumped it, shaking the excess water off.

"It's my job," he answered with a smile.

"Aww, thanks so much, you're a champ!" Charlotte dropped onto the back seat heavily with her backpack, umbrella and smaller bag, sighing happily. Looking to her left at Antonio, who had moved over for her, she smiled goofily, then realised two little faces staring at her inquisitively from the opposite seats. She gasped with delight. "Hello there! I'm Charlotte!"

The smallest girl smiled shyly, held a stuffed toy rabbit close to her face and slid behind her big sister's elbow.

"Hello, Charlotte, my name is Olivia Maria Sanchez. I'm seven, nearly eight years old. It's very nice to meet you. This is my little sister, Bella. She's shy. Her rabbit's name is Poncho."

Charlotte laughed. "Delighted to meet you, Olivia, Bella... and hello, Poncho! What beautiful names! Now I heard something about jumping in puddles earlier... is this true? Am I in the company of fellow puddle-jumping fans?" Charlotte kept a straight face but could hear Antonio chuckling next to her.

"It was Poncho's idea!" blurted Bella from behind her sister.

"Ahh, I see. Sometimes, rabbits can have very fun ideas, but they can get you into trouble. I don't currently have a rabbit, but I jumped in the puddles all the same." She lowered her voice to a whisper. "So I have no excuse at all... just have a wet bum."

The little girls squealed with laughter, and Bella held out Poncho as if to face his accusation publicly.

"My goodness, Charlotte, our manners!" said Antonio. "Would you like a towel? We do have a spare here somewhere. Hugo, do you know if there's another towel in the back?"

The intercom spluttered and Hugo answered a few moments later.

"I'm sorry, Sir, I believe we've used both towels for the girls. I am happy to grab some more, should our guest require one."

Charlotte waved her hands in protest. "No, no, I'm fine guys, honestly all good! I've got a change of clothes and spare thongs in my bag!"

The girls squealed again along with another surprised laugh from Antonio.

Charlotte glanced between their faces, confused as to what was so funny. When it finally dawned on her, she smiled and nodded. "Ahh, got it. Sorry, thong means something else here, doesn't it! I meant these thingos!" She took off both sandals and pretended to alligator-snap at the giggling girls. Charlotte heard a loud sneeze through the intercom. The driver, Hugo, was suffering from a nasty cold.

"Hugo, mate, if you've caught a cold because of letting me in the car, I'll never forgive myself. Do you need a Strepsil?"

The intercom crackled. "Uh... thank you, Miss... what is a Strepsil?"

Charlotte rummaged inside her bag. "It's one of these, matey," she said, holding up the box. "For coughs and colds, they're good stuff."

"Thank you, Miss, but I'm fine. I appreciate your kindness."

Charlotte could just make out Hugo blowing his nose with one hand through the glass. She furrowed her brow, unconvinced, holding the medicated cough drops on her lap just in case.

"So, what are you guys up to today?" Charlotte asked the girls enthusiastically, conscious of Antonio looking at her.

I can't look at him... don't look at how gorgeous he is, just sitting there, couple of buttons open on his shirt, that tanned, muscular chest.... STOP! Just focus on his kids.

"We're going to work, with Papa!" Olivia said, her little face beaming. "We get to play on the set and play dress ups, we're going to wear costumes!"

"Oh my goodness, that's awesome! How fun does that sound? And hey, if we have time and your papa says it's okay, you could come visit me in the make-up department and we could do some face painting! What do you think?" She turned to look at Antonio and fell instantly entranced by his deep brown eyes again. He had a faint smile and a look of slight incredulity on his face.

The little girls were yelling excitedly. "Can you make me look like a unicorn?" Bella asked, perched on the edge of her seat.

"Charlotte, could you please do a cat face on me?" Olivia asked excitedly.

Antonio leaned towards Charlotte, and she felt her head swim with his scent. "Every day, she asks if we can get a cat."

Charlotte laughed softly, trying to mask the attraction she felt towards Antonio, who shuffled forward, ushering his youngest backwards on her seat.

"My Bella, you need to put your seatbelt back on, please, sit back. We can see if Charlotte has some free time a little later; she is a very busy lady... plus her boss is a *'rezongón,'* he said gruffly before tickling the girls, making them both squeal again. He fussed over his youngest and clicked on her seatbelt.

What a lovely father he is... so caring... so... nice smelling.... Dammit, snap out of it, Grant!

They soon arrived at the studio, and Hugo pulled up outside the main building where all the executives and assistants kept busy. It always seemed like a beehive to Charlotte. As she opened the limo door and climbed out the opposite side, Hugo frantically raced around to assist her.

Charlotte patted Hugo on the arm and passed him the cough drops. "Here you go, my friend. Please take these, I'll feel less guilty. They'll hopefully clear out your shnozz and make your throat feel better. Hey, and at least it's stopped raining now!"

Hugo put a hand on his heart and looked at Charlotte, almost amazed. "Mr Sanchez said you were lovely, and now I see what he means. Thank you, Miss Charlotte," he said earnestly, stifling another little cough.

Geez mate, it's only a three-dollar pack of Strepsils, I'm not giving you a freakin' kidney.

"All good, Mr Hugo! I'm sure I'll see ya around!" She made her way around to the sidewalk, where Antonio and his girls were standing. She threw her stuff aside and crouched, hands on knees.

"Now, Miss Trouble One and Miss Trouble Two; I will see you later today, okay? Please come and visit me, if you can. You will be transformed into unicorns and cats. I hope you have a super fun day!"

To her surprise, the little girls launched at her, giving her a big hug from each side.

"Aww, thank you so much! I needed those cuddles!"

They giggled and ran off towards the automatic doors, adorned with tiny backpacks, Poncho flying around wildly as Bella ran full pelt towards the entrance.

Charlotte laughed and stood with a hand over her mouth. "Antonio, your girls are just perfection... what little angels!" she said, watching as they climbed over one of the squat couches in the lobby area.

Antonio smiled as he stood next to Charlotte and watched his kids scuttle off.

She became very conscious of his shoulder touching hers, arousing her senses.

"They are lovely girls... but then I am biased." He suddenly turned to her. "Will you please have dinner with me tonight?"

Charlotte felt like she'd been plunged into icy cold water. Her lungs filled rapidly, eyes widened, and she turned slowly to face him, stuttering as she did so. "I... um... wha..."

"I know Amanda has that stupid rule, and I don't want to make trouble for you... we can easily say it's a work meeting. I can pick you up later from your apartment so no one will see us?"

Charlotte continued to stutter and blink repeatedly. His eyes were burning with intensity. His stubbled chin, those beautiful lips. She wanted to kiss him and say yes to anything he asked of her. She eventually reclaimed her voice and blurted out the first thing that popped into her mind. "I'm already going out on a date tonight!"

Antonio nodded sadly and looked at the ground. "Liam. You're going out on a date with Liam, aren't you?"

Charlotte couldn't speak at first, but her mouth continued to open and close like a goldfish, entirely of its own accord. "Yes, how did you guess?"

"Call it a hunch. The other night, at the bar, I wanted to ask if you'd like to come to Disneyland. With me and the girls. We were given summer passes, through the studio. But it's okay, you're probably not interested-"

"No! I would LOVE to come to Disneyland! Do you mean like, as an assistant, or nanny for the girls or something?"

Where the hell did that come from? Charlotte you idiot.

Antonio's brow furrowed. "As a... what? No, not as staff, as our guest, Charlotte! As my... as a family guest. My girls clearly love you, within five seconds of meeting you. They are a great judge of character."

Oh no, he looks hurt... like a little scolded puppy... why can't I filter my big stupid mouth.

Charlotte took a deep, steadying breath. "Yes, Antonio. I would love to accompany you. Name the day and time, and I will be there." She attempted to quell the excited screaming in her head.

Antonio looked back up at her, and for a split second the happiness on his face made Charlotte believe he was about to embrace her.

He cleared his throat and regained his composure. "Excellent. Olivia and Bella will be very happy. I told them you were from Australia, so they've been fairly restrained so far with asking questions about kangaroos and koalas, but I don't think I can hold them off forever."

A strand of dark hair fell in his eyes again, and as he shook his head, Charlotte realised how beautiful this man was. There was such a deep sadness beneath the surface, and she just wanted to hold him and soothe his pain. He didn't seem to realise how amazing he was, what power he commanded, though his humility just added to the charm. Realising she was unabashedly staring, Charlotte shook her head. "Anyway, time for me to go! Better not be late for Voss the Boss. Hope you have a great day. Hopefully see you guys later!" She scooped up her bags and umbrella awkwardly.

He stood and smiled at her, waving as she walked away.

A distant shout made Charlotte look back.

"Bye Charlotte!" Bella was yelling and waving while clinging to her father's leg.

Charlotte laughed, blew a kiss and waved back before walking around a corner. As soon as she was out of sight, she dropped her stuff and leaned against the side of the building.

What... the... bloody... hell... so Charlotte, you're going on a date with Liam Reeves tonight. Then you're going to Disneyland on the weekend with Antonio freakin' Sanchez and his kids. How many times over is your boss going to kill you? Exactly how big of a death wish do you actually have?

She looked up and saw crew members looking at her with puzzled expressions. As usual, no one stopped to ask if she was alright. But this time, it suited her just fine.

The morning raced by in a blur. They were nearing the end of filming for the first series and the pressure, if possible, had been turned up another notch. Amanda had them on a brutal schedule where bathroom breaks were now a luxury, let alone a chance to eat anything. Berating became so commonplace that the words didn't even compute with Charlotte anymore. They were constantly "too slow" and "so useless" and "a waste of money" and blah blah blah.

"I am losing too much weight, all my clothes are hanging off me," Zephyr whined as they finished up an impressive-looking gash over an actor's cheek.

Tess rolled her eyes at Charlotte, who'd just looked up from her side of the make-up room. "Cry me a river, you skinny little asshole," she muttered under her breath.

Charlotte snorted with laughter, causing Zephyr to glare menacingly at the pair of them.

Tess had become so incredibly important to Charlotte as a trusted friend, confidante and all-round kindred-spirit. Charlotte felt more than anyone that Amanda was scrutinising her behaviour the most, and Tess felt it her duty to protect her. Charlotte was immeasurably grateful for this and wasn't sure how she would be coping in this environment without her or anyone to watch her back.

Due to the increasing number of male crew members hanging around Charlotte for no reason, Amanda's surveillance became increasingly intrusive by the day. As she walked into the make-up room with a face like thunder, Amanda's gaze would have lasered through steel as she stomped over to Charlotte's side.

Don't make eye contact... don't make eye contact.

"Charlotte, just a reminder, as you've probably forgotten: my 'screw the crew' rule is hard and fast. No discussion, no hesitation.

I find you fraternising with anyone we work with, and I will fire you in a heartbeat. You'll never get another job in this town again. Clear?"

Charlotte stood up straight, stretched and smiled sweetly at Amanda. Unbeknownst to her boss, from her vantage point, she could see Antonio and the kids making their way to the makeup room.

Screw it. Let's have some fun.

"Fraternising? That's a thirty-point word right there, boss!"

Charlotte could hear collective gasps from her coworkers.

Amanda's jaw dropped.

"Auntie Charlotte!!" yelled the girls in unison as they ran towards her.

"Little beans! Hello! How is your day going? Are you having fun?" She hugged the girls with one arm each, pulling them into her ribcage. Looking up from her crouched position, she saw Amanda's face contort in horror and the handsome, beaming face of Antonio standing right behind her.

Charlotte matched the warmth of his smile and continued to get squeezed by the little girls.

"Auntie Charlotte, we saw so many things!" said Bella. "There was a horse, and I saw a scary poster with eyeballs, and we dressed up like old ladies, and I saw a sparkly bird!"

Charlotte laughed but was conscious of all the eyes in the room on her right now.

"That sounds so cool! Did Poncho dress up like an old lady, too? Wear little high heels and have a handbag?" She pretended to hold a purse with her hands. Bella leaned against Charlotte and barked with laughter.

"Rabbits don't wear shoes or carry old lady stuff, Auntie Charlotte."

"Oh, of course they don't, how silly of me."

"Can you paint our faces now please?" Olivia pleaded.

Charlotte looked up at Antonio, who had a dreamy look on his face, then to Amanda, who's expression looked like it had been plastered onto her face with one of their prosthetic kits.

"Is it okay if I take ten minutes, boss? Just to turn *this* little lady into a cat and *this* little lady into a unicorn?"

Amanda's lips stretched over her teeth until she looked sideways at Antonio.

"Of course you can spend your lunch break with these little angels, *Auntie* Charlotte." As the girls jumped up and down with excitement, Charlotte stood up and saw Amanda's eyes morph into venomous slits.

"Speaking of lunch, have you eaten anything today, Charlotte?" asked Antonio. "The catering table is full. Do you want me to bring you a plate of sandwiches or wraps?"

"That would be so amazing, thank you! Could you bring some for Tess and Zephyr as well? We've been so flat out!"

"Sure."

As Amanda's head whipped round, Antonio's expression changed into an amenable grin. "Amanda, you want to come help us get some lunch for your hard workers?" he asked cheerily.

"Uh... yes, of course, Antonio," she said and made her way towards the door. Antonio ushered her out, and as she walked ahead of him, he turned back and winked at Charlotte.

She stifled a laugh. He was definitely having fun with this, and although Charlotte was certain she'd cop it later, she had to admit, it was worth it. Luckily, Amanda was absent for the rest of the day. Uncertain whether this was Antonio's doing or not, Charlotte, and she was certain the rest of the crew, were grateful for the space. Having had something to eat, albeit wolfed down, and no micromanager looming over their shoulders, made for a happier and more productive afternoon.

As they were cleaning up after another ten-hour day, Tess leaned in with her broom to where Charlotte was tidying up the prosthetics counter. "Girl, isn't tonight your date with you-know-who?" she asked quietly.

They both suspected Zephyr would rat them out in a split second to Amanda given half the chance, so secrecy was imperative.

Charlotte could see Zephyr looking over but trying to act like they weren't listening.

"Correct! This is the 'nerdy-cafe' guy though. The other guy is a bit of a dickhead, so I've called it off. To be honest, I'm so tired. I might just cancel this one, too. I can't be arsed."

Charlotte saw Tess's brow unfurrow as she comprehended what was going on and winked. "Girl, you gotta go, come on now. What does the nerdy guy do again?" Tess spoke slightly louder than before, her eyes darting to the side mischievously.

"I think he's a chef or works in a kitchen or something. Has the big black horned-rimmed glasses? We just talked about food while I was waiting for our coffees. I dunno though."

"You have to have something else besides work, Charlotte. I got my kids and my mom, Amanda travels back to Hades on her broomstick, Zephyr has... whatever stupid spy shit Zephyr does at night, who cares."

"I heard that!" said Zephyr.

Charlotte peered around Tess and laughed.

"I'll go home and have a shower, see how I feel after that," said Charlotte. "I'll text you."

"Okay. But I think you should go. Tell me all about it okay, girl? I need some excitement in my life, so I'm gonna live vicariously through you," She grabbed the cloth Charlotte was holding and flicked it at her bottom. "Now, get out of here, I'll finish this. Git!"

Charlotte thought about protesting but saw the clock read 7pm. To be ready in time, she'd need to leave right now. Pulling Tess into a hug, she thanked her, then yelled goodbye to Zephyr, who reciprocated with a grunt.

She grabbed her bags, ran out the door and banged into the doorframe as she turned back to retrieve her umbrella. Bags flying off one shoulder, she attempted to wave goodbye but by doing so hit the wall and left a mark from the umbrella's handle.

"Oh... whoopsies," she grimaced, seeing Tess laughing and shaking her head.

Charlotte's phone pinged at 7:58pm, signalling a text message. Toothbrush protruding from her mouth, hair curling iron in one hand and fresh underwear in the other, she threw her knickers down on the bed and pressed the screen to read the text:

Hey, Aussie girl, I'm outside. Come down when you're ready. Liam x

Crap! He's early! Liam Reeves is early. That will just never, ever, not sound weird.

Charlotte threw on a black, halter-neck dress she thought suited the occasion, and awkwardly pulled on one high heel. Hobbling back to the bathroom, she spat into the sink and wiped her mouth. Leaning into the mirror, she drew some lip pencil and applied some lipstick. Her hair was now lopsided curl-wise, so she pinned one side up. It felt nice to have it loose instead of tied back for a change. Squirting on some perfume, she stood back and appraised herself as barely date-worthy.

She grabbed her phone and a small handbag she'd bought from a thrift shop, stuffing in various things she might need for the night.

8:03pm. Time to go.

As she slammed the front door to her building, she turned around to see a ginormous white limousine parked in front of her. Liam was standing through the top window, leaning on the roof. He had a big bunch of red roses and a huge grin on his face.

She gasped. "Holy shit!"

"Nice to see you, too, Aussie girl. Ready for some fun?" His large cheeky grin made her smile.

Two limo rides in one day. What would Kev and Mave say to that?

Charlotte had to admit she was nervous. Suddenly aware of her hands and how they couldn't stop fidgeting with the straps of her handbag, she attempted to make polite and normal conversation in the cavernous vehicle as they travelled.

"Hey, would you like a drink, Charlotte?" Liam asked from the seat opposite her.

Even if she slouched and stretched out her legs, she wouldn't reach his feet with hers. It was like sitting at one of those long dinner tables, where one had to get up just to pass the salt.

Thing is, these people don't have to get up. They have salt-passerers to do that kinda stuff for them.

"Yeah, thanks, that would be grouse!"

"Ahh, so she's a scotch whisky fan, nice, nice," he said as he poured a small bottle of amber liquid into a heavy glass tumbler and added some ice with a little set of tongs. "Here you go."

Unsure of what she'd just requested, Charlotte took the glass with thanks. Taking a sip, she wondered momentarily if he had mistakenly poured turpentine instead of whisky.

"So, is this your limo, or do you guys like, rent them out?" she asked with a raspy voice, the harsh liquor clawing at her throat.

Liam snorted. "No, it's my limo, honey. It's like a package of stuff you get when you become famous."

"Wow... so what else is in the package? Like shampoo and soap?"

"Yeah, if I didn't get a soap-rope after *Wonderstuff*, there would have been hell to pay!"

"Ahh, I see. Hey, so where are we going?"

"We're going to this tiny Italian restaurant in the Hills. It's like someone's family house. None of the staff speak any English, it's great. The food is to die for, they just bring it to you, no menus. They don't advertise, you just have to know people." He winked.

"Blimey! So no one there will know Amanda? I'm shitting myself she'll find out, mate, honestly, there's bricks in my undies."

Liam leaned towards her, his gaze seductive. "Do not worry, Aussie girl. I got you. And your undies."

They arrived shortly at their destination, which was hard to see through the darkened windows, especially at night. Charlotte could just make out a man wearing a waistcoat standing on the sidewalk in a normal looking, albeit fancy, suburban street. The houses were sizable, on huge plots of land.

Liam's driver, who seemed a lot less sweet than Hugo, opened the car door and she thanked him. He looked stoically ahead, not seeming to notice she was even there.

"Buonasera, signorina, Buonasera, signor Reeves," the man in the waistcoat said. He gestured towards the front door, then walked quickly ahead of them.

Charlotte felt Liam's hand on the small of her back, gently guiding her to walk in front of him, making her skin tingle.

As they walked inside the warm, dimly lit entrance, they were met by another man wearing a waistcoat, who smiled and ushered them into one of the rooms off the main hallway. Charlotte couldn't see any other diners, and the rooms they passed were of varying sizes–just like a normal house with its furniture cleared out. She took in her surroundings. Candles burned inside little jars on top of tables with red checkered tablecloths, deep red walls and ornate, white decorated freezes on the high ceilings framed crystal light fittings. A heavenly smell of Italian food wafted through the venue, and she felt her stomach rumble in response.

"Signorina," said one of the waiters as he stood behind a pulled-out chair.

Charlotte reciprocated his smile and sat down, taking in more of the little room. There was an old oak cabinet and a small bar, beautifully carved from a dark wood of some kind.

"Shit, I feel just like Lady and the Tramp," Charlotte exclaimed, hand on her heart as she looked around.

Liam laughed. "Well, hopefully a little more upscale than sitting outside with dogs, at least," he joked as a waiter unfolded a crisp white linen napkin and placed it on his lap.

"So, we don't order? How do we know what we're eating?"

"Nope, just enjoy, and hopefully you're not allergic to anything they bring out!"

Charlotte smiled to herself, thinking she hadn't really been asked any specific food-related questions by her date. She was unaware of any prevailing food allergies, but Liam didn't know that.

"So, Aussie girl, now that we can talk properly, what do you think of Hollywood? Your coworkers, your work, your team? Is it what you expected?" A waiter poured red wine into his glass.

Charlotte looked around surreptitiously, furrowing her brow and ignoring his questions. "Sorry, um, where are all the other people? I'm looking over my shoulder like Amanda's going to be there... but *no one* is there!"

Liam smirked. "I hired the entire place for the night. So *no one* is going to be behind you."

"Oh my God! Liam, are you serious? That's really sweet! Holy shit! Liam Reeves bought out a restaurant for little old me."

"Well, I didn't *buy* it... I mean, I *could*... but..." he said with a smug head wobble.

Charlotte chuckled politely.

I can't quite place this guy. Is it sweetness? Or just pure arrogance?

"So, to answer your question: Hollywood is... interesting. I think I mentioned the other night when we were playing pool, the place I'm from is *tiny*. Like, it's dusty, hot and there's one main street. I don't think anyone here could pronounce it, either."

Liam sat back and looked at the ceiling, narrowing his eyes in thought. "I'm thinking like, a Mad Max landscape where you drive down to get milk in a souped-up Mario-cart with flames shooting out the back... sawn-off shotgun strapped around your chest?"

"Yeah, just like that. I've got a massive electric guitar on the top that I have my gimp play while driving a hundred kilometres an hour down Sheridan Street."

"Cool. That's just your average weekday, or a special occasion?"

"No, just your everyday. While wearing my Ugs."

Their easy banter was interrupted by the arrival of two plates of food, delivered by two very handsome waiters who announced the dishes in fast-flowing Italian.

Charlotte looked over at Liam and frowned. "I don't speak Italian, do you know what he said?"

"No idea. I had to learn some for one of my drama movies, but I was pretty lousy at languages to be honest."

"Ahh, well, we can't be good at everything! Looks good, smells good, let's give it a red-hot crack!" Charlotte stabbed one of the doughy-looking parcels on her plate.

"It's gnocchi! Aww, if only Kev was here to see this."

"Who's Kev?"

"He's my old boss... but more like my dad. As in, the dad I would have chosen for myself. He's awesome. Him and his wife Mave are like my favourite people on earth." To her surprise, tears quickly filled her eyes.

"You miss them, huh?"

"Yes. Every damn day."

Liam reached over the tablecloth and took her hand, smiling sweetly.

"Our loved ones are always with us in spirit, Charlotte."

"Thanks, Liam," she said, sniffling and wiping her eyes. "Geez, I didn't think I'd get all emotional over an entrée, what the hell's that all about eh?"

"There's something I've been wanting to do since the first time when you turned my face into a bloody mess. If you'll permit me?" He got up and walked around to her.

"What?" Charlotte exclaimed as she looked up at him, wiping her nose with the back of her hand.

Liam laughed, cupped her face and leaned down to kiss her tenderly on the mouth. It was only brief, but Charlotte felt her head spin. She opened her eyes and saw him smiling at her, his kind hazel eyes sparkling in the subdued light. She giggled, despite herself, and placed her fingers over her mouth as he sat again.

"Liam Reeves just kissed me," she said with a giggle, then snorted loudly.

Liam laughed and shook his head, reaching for his glass of wine.

"You're one of a kind, Charlotte, that's for sure."

A never-ending stream of courses comprised of various dishes prepared in every way imaginable came their way throughout the pleasant evening. Seafood, beef, chicken, vegetables, all small plates like tapas and each exploding with flavour. Wines changed regularly, and Charlotte could barely keep track of what she was eating or drinking.

Their dishwasher deserves a bloody salary raise, that's for certain.

Looking at her watch, Charlotte swore when she realised how late it was. "Matey, this has been so much fun, but I gotta go get some sleep. Tomorrow, it's just Tess and me doing all the retakes, since Zephyr is away."

"That's a shame. I had one more activity in mind before we parted ways," he said, looking at her from under his arched eyebrows, smiling mischievously.

Charlotte cocked her head and chuckled. "Mate, you may be super famous but I ain't droppin' these knickers after one date—sozballs."

"Ahh, nuts. I thought the flowers would have sealed the deal."

"They were lovely. This has been *lovely*. You are lovely. Now can we split the bill? Or will I need to take out a bank loan for that?"

"If you have a spare fifteen grand lying around, we can split it."

"Holy shit! Are you serious?"

"Yeah."

"Okay... well, how about I take *you* out next time? I'll take you on a 'Gundagai experience' right here in Hollywood. Deal?"

Liam laughed. "Deal, Aussie girl."

As the limo pulled up outside her apartment building, Charlotte could feel her heavy eyelids drooping.

Liam switched seats and was now sitting right next to her, their shoulders touching. She suddenly became aware of his body heat and male scent. The combination resulted in a heady cocktail, and she could feel her own body questioning the decision she'd made not to take things further tonight.

"You're really special, Charlotte," he said quietly, turning sideways in the seat and taking her head in his hands. Slowly and seductively, he drew her, their lips gently meeting. What started off as tender quickly turned into a passionate and heated exchange, with Liam's hands sliding down to her chest and back. Charlotte instinctively grabbed the hand on her right breast and diverted it elsewhere.

Damn, Liam Reeves is a good kisser. Hummunah.

"So, can I come upstairs with you?" he whispered, nibbling at her neck.

She let out a little moan as his tongue circled around her collarbone.

No... yeah... no, definitely not... but maybe... gah, my brain and britches are not agreeing on this one. What about Antonio?

"No, Liam. I'm sorry but this is going too fast for me. I gotta go now. Thank you for a truly wonderful evening." She untangled herself from him and composed herself. Taking a deep breath and smiling at her date, she went to open the limo door before it opened for her.

I don't think I'm ever going to get used to this.

"You're welcome, Aussie girl," he said through the window as the chauffeur returned to the driver's side. "I'll be waiting for your invite. I'm already looking forward to date number two: The 'Goondergay Experience.'"

Charlotte walked up the stairs to her front door, turned the key in the lock and looked back to wave. The limo drove off, she heard the door lock behind her, then made her way back up to her apartment.

Turning on the light, she went over to the kettle and switched it on. She needed a cup of tea and a sit down to process one of the most amazing dates she'd ever experienced.

Thirty thousand dollars for a date? FARK!

Normally, she'd have been very happy with a Hawaiian parma and a couple of beers from the Criterion, let alone all this malarkey. She had never been able to take a date to her own pub, lest the poor bloke would have been ridiculed beyond belief.

Dating an extremely famous and ridiculously gorgeous movie star at a pricey restaurant all to themselves? *Pig's arse.* And what was worse, she couldn't tell anyone. Mave and Kev wouldn't know who Liam was, and none of her friends back home would ever believe her. Tess was the only person she could confide in. Maybe they could sneak off tomorrow for five minutes, and she could tell her about it. Or was it too late to text?

Rummaging around in her little bag, she found her phone. It buzzed, notifying her she'd received a call from an unknown number. She called voicemail and listened to the message:

"Hey, Charlotte, it's Antonio. Just wanted to let you know I've been thinking about you, a lot. I know you're not supposed to date coworkers, and Amanda's rules, I know... but anyway, would you consider coming to Disneyland as my date? Please just think about it, no pressure. We're all looking forward to seeing you again, the girls won't stop asking about you. We're all a little smitten. (cough) Ah, well I'm rambling now. Okay, bye. See you at work tomorrow. Bye. Again."

Holy, freakin' crap-balls.

CHAPTER 10

"He said what?" Tess whispered incredulously as they hid in the park together early the next morning.

Charlotte walked away, then turned back, passing by Tess, then spun on her heel and came back. "I know. He wants me to come to Disneyland as his *date*. I didn't know, I thought it was just because of the kids... oh I don't know... maybe I did know... but now I've gone and pashed Liam... shit! Tess, I'm in trouble."

"Girl, stop pacing, you're making me dizzy! Okay, it's alright, we can figure this out. So, I gotta ask first. Liam: good kisser? I'm guessing that's what 'pashed' means?"

"Tess, that is *not* the most important thing happening here! Focus!"

Tess dipped her chin and raised her eyebrows at Charlotte, who sighed and slumped her shoulders.

"Amay-zing kisser," she mouthed.

Tess smiled and closed her eyes, as if savouring the thought. "Mm, mm... for a rich white boy, he's pretty fine, I gotta say. Nice ass?"

"Tess!"

"Okay, okay. I know it's fine, I've looked, you don't have to tell me. So, date with Liam, you've kissed him... just kissing?"

Charlotte cocked her head, then nodded.

"Just checking, just checking. Okay, so one date down with Liam, another planned. We've also got the Disneyland date with Antonio and his kids. Is there anyone else coming with you? And has anything happened with Antonio? You kissed him?"

Charlotte sighed loudly and looked up at the sky. "No, I bloody wish. Those eyes... that hair... the way he smells... oh my."

Tess took a sip of her coffee, watching Charlotte as she swooned. "Okay, how about this for a plan: you go with the Sanchez gang, kiss Antonio... oh, don't look at me like that, you have to! Then you weigh it up. Antonio might be a terrible kisser, which means he's probably terrible in bed. Liam is known for liking the ladies though, so he's probably had a lotta practice with both."

"Yeah, I can imagine he just wants an Aussie bogan notch on his belt."

"A what?"

"Never mind."

"The point is, honey, you got these two guys, plus more if you wanted, eating out of your hand. It comes down to what *you* want. You just want fun? I'd date Liam for a while, get the full 'Hollywood experience' with a movie star. But just know that by proxy you'd be sleeping with half of the town, the way that boy gets around. Now Antonio... gorgeous, but he's coming through the other side of a messy divorce, so he's fragile. Super powerful though, he holds a lot of weight around here. He's a really nice guy, just needs a bit more... backbone, assertiveness, I think. Also, his ex-wife... well, wife? No one knows if they've formally split. Damn, she makes Amanda look like a walk in the park. Either way, girl, you're playing with fire, and with these two harpies in play, one can ruin your career, the other will rip your head off. You gotta be smart about this. So, it all comes down to what you want, Char? You want a fling, or a potential relationship baptised in flames?"

At that moment, a small truck drove past, its noisy brakes squeaking as it came to a stop. Charlotte was mesmerised as she looked at the side of the truck, watching a delivery guy get out and open the back doors. Two eagles faced each other, their wings spread across the company name: *Eagle refrigerated foods. Eagles...*

"Yo, Char, you listening to me?" Tess barked, patting Charlotte on the arm.

She jumped. "Shit, Tess, yes, sorry, I... it was just..."

"Good morning, lovely ladies, how are you doing?" asked a familiar voice, appearing out of nowhere. Charlotte spun around to see Antonio ambling towards them under the tree. He wore a dark blue business shirt that contrasted beautifully with his olive-brown skin. His dark eyes sparkled in the dappled sunlight, and that pesky strand of fringe played over his forehead. How she wanted to run her hands through his hair and play with that fringe.

"Hi," Charlotte answered dopily.

"Hey," he responded, reciprocating her wide smile.

Far away, Charlotte heard Tess clear her throat.

"Uh, hey, you two—just a heads up: Amanda is coming this way, so you might both wanna, you know, come back to planet *earth*."

Charlotte tucked her hair behind her ear and took a sip from her coffee cup.

Antonio coughed, started rolling up his shirt sleeves and looked up to address the approaching woman.

"Ahh, Amanda, I'm glad I caught you, good morning! I was just talking to the girls about the reshoots today. Edward Meeks and I wanted Charlotte to spend some time with us in the green-screen room. Would that be okay with you?" There was a determination in his voice that Charlotte hadn't heard before; it seemed much more assertive as opposed to his usual soothing purr.

"Are you trying to steal my staff again, Antonio?" she asked, batting her long, sparkling eyelashes and smiling sweetly through gritted teeth. Her eyes darted to Charlotte and narrowed menacingly. "Why Charlotte; she doesn't know anything? Why not take Tess, who's more experienced?"

Antonio calmly finished rolling his sleeves and put his hands on his hips. By doing so, Charlotte could see sideways through his shirt over his muscular torso. She quickly looked away and sipped her coffee.

"Exactly for that reason. We want to show Charlotte how the process works. Don't you want your staff to develop and grow? She can help you more after receiving some training."

All eyes were on Amanda, and although Charlotte sorely wished she wasn't the topic of this conversation, it was nice to see Amanda caught on the back foot, watching as she stuttered and brushed her cheek with long, colourful claw-like fingernails.

"Of course. I want nothing but the best for my staff, Antonio. But... we need all hands on deck today as there's only the two of them working. Can we compromise, and I get her back in the afternoon? But you're the boss, obviously. If you want Charlotte, *you can have her.*"

If looks could kill, Charlotte was certain she'd have been melted by the hatred blazing from Amanda's eyes.

What, the actual...

"Cool, then it's settled. Tess, I'm sorry to leave you flying solo this morning, my dear! We'll have Charlotte back to you after lunch, okay?" Antonio leaned over and patted Tess on the arm.

"It's all good, I'll hold down the fort," Tess said, giving Charlotte a little wink.

"Thanks so much, to both of you. Shall we, Charlotte?"

Charlotte grabbed her backpack off the ground. "I... um... okay, oh, thank you, Amanda, uh... Tess, I'll see you later, k?" She squeezed Tess's hand as she passed and followed Antonio, already striding away from her, bag in hand. Charlotte desperately hoped Tess wouldn't have to endure any wrath as a result of the director's bizarre decision... thinking it was best not to look back. As she jogged to catch up with Antonio, she saw Hugo standing beside the back of the limo, happy to see his smiling face.

"Hugo, matey! Hey, how are you feeling, any better?"

"Much improved, thank you, Miss Charlotte," he said demurely, his expression betraying his twinkling eyes. "Your *Strepseel*, they helped me greatly."

"Aww, so glad to hear that, yay!" she said as she followed Antonio into the back of the limousine, awkwardly trying to manoeuvre herself into a seat so her bag didn't go flying in front of her. Unfortunately, by doing so, she hit her head hard on the roof, causing Hugo, Antonio and two other men in the limousine to fuss over her, asking if she was okay.

"Scchhkk, ow! Ya mother frack—bloody limos!!" She sucked in her breath and held her throbbing forehead as she landed in the back seat.

"There's our girl, as demure as ever."

Charlotte saw Meeks suddenly crouching in front of her, his hand gently touching her head.

"Meeksy! Is that actually you, or am I just seeing mega-stars?"

The passengers erupted with laughter. Meeks handed Charlotte a napkin wrapped around some ice, and she sat back on the seat. It felt soothing as she gently placed it on her head.

"Oh, I've missed you, kiddo. Not sure if you can see properly with the ring of tweety-birds, but we've got a couple of friends in the car. Brian from Universal on a phone call whom you met the other night, and Jake Hardy from HBO."

Charlotte's one open eye bulged. "Jake? Holy shit! Jake from the plane ride?"

"Charlotte! Haha! Hello, I was wondering whether this make-up artist prodigy I've been hearing about was the same superwoman! And here you are!"

"Not so super right now, with a massive freakin' egg on my head, but the same clutz you met in the sky! How are ya, mate? Hey, how's it goin' Brian?"

He smiled and waved at her, still engaged in his phone call.

Charlotte heard a quiet cough to her right and realised Hugo was still standing there, next to the open door.

"Is Miss Charlotte alright? Can I assist before we depart?"

"Oh, Hugo, matey, thank you. I'm just an idiot, that's not going to change. Please, fire on."

Hugo looked confused.

"We're okay to depart now, Hugo, thanks," Antonio said.

Hugo nodded and shut the door gently.

"Antonio and I were giving these gentlemen a lift, chatting about a new project. Ant, gotta say, well done on extracting Charlotte from Amanda's clutches; that couldn't have been easy."

Antonio puffed out his chest and pointed his thumbs inward.

"Char, honey, we're jamming about this new series... just thinking of people who we want on the project group. It'll be pretty small, intimate and kinda intense. Question: would you be keen to be *on* camera, or stick to the make-up artistry?"

Charlotte let her hand fall down to her lap and found her lip curling involuntarily. "Wah? You're thinking of me, in *front* of the camera? You insane? I'd trash the joint... plus, I can't act to save my life."

Meeks laughed and shook his head, then looked across at Jake, also chuckling.

"Your reaction is the exact reason we want you, Char. We're looking for realism, and it doesn't get much more real than you, my darling."

"Fark, mate, how hard did I hit my head?"

"It's okay, we can talk about it later and I can go through some more details with you, but please think about it, okay?"

"Okay... I mean, I'm willing to give anything a go, just don't want to waste the studio's time and money."

Meeks smiled and looked across at Jake.

"You're right, Meeks," said Jake. "She's a rare gem. How often do we hear that?"

Although Charlotte's head had stopped throbbing from the collision, it was still spinning with all the new people and processes she was being exposed to. Just when she was becoming comfortable with her new career in a new and very different place, she was now being dragged out of the nice little comfort zone she'd managed to create.

Antonio and Meeks stayed very close to Charlotte and were, as usual, receptive to her questions and comments about the reshoot process and what post-production would look like. They went through what happened after the make-up artists completed their tasks step by step, so it all started to make more sense to her. She couldn't remember everyone's names, so had to resort to the usual nickname game she often played in her head. 'Bad-breath Billy' and 'No-neck Nick' were perfectly nice guys; she just made a mental note never to play the game out loud.

When they'd watched some footage together and Charlotte had noted the prosthetics and make-up improvements she'd want to look at, it had reached late morning.

Meeks had needed to duck out to speak with someone and mentioned he'd be back soon to meet them for an early lunch. With only a few minutes in between, Antonio asked Charlotte to follow him into one of the green-screen rooms, which was fairly small and brimming with equipment.

"Char, this is where you'd spend a fair bit of time if you were working on Brian's horror franchise, one of the projects we wanted you to join."

Char. He hadn't called her that before; it felt warming and endearing. She looked at Antonio in the semi-darkness and a thought suddenly hit her.

I am dead-set, head over heels, fair-dinkum in love with this man.

Her lungs inflated suddenly, as if she'd been plunged into icy water. She felt flutters in her chest, a restriction in her throat, feeling like they were in a bubble together, just the two of them were left in the world.

A little voice in the back of her head, perhaps the logical voice of reason, said she barely knew him. Although they'd had some great conversations and she knew he was a kind, considerate person, there were still a lot of unknown factors. And the sobering fact he was still technically married and very much off-limits in every way.

"... And, of course, it's expensive, haha."

Charlotte heard Antonio joke when the fog in her brain subsided, and she started to listen.

"Hmm...."

"Char, are you okay? Oh no, have I been talking too fast? I'm being too Spanish again, aren't I? We are known for talking too much, too fast. It's just because I am trying to impress you." He chuckled.

"Yeah, no... you're all good... it's, um...." Suddenly aware of how close they were standing, and the heat she could feel coming from his body, she stepped back. His olive-skinned, muscular, delectable body with a butt she wanted to bite filled her vision.

He turned slowly to face her. "Charlotte... did you get my message last night?" he asked quietly, eyes smouldering.

"Yeah, I did."

"I... I'm sorry... I hope I'm not bothering you... I just... you're..."

The energy between them was palpable, and Charlotte was aware she was breathing heavily. She looked down from their locked eyes and could see his broad chest rapidly rising and falling. Her hand reached out to comfort him, and as she moved closer to touch his shoulder, his intoxicating scent instinctively forced her eyes to close. She opened them again briefly to see his handsome face come closer, then felt his lips make contact with hers. They were soft, sweet, and smooth, contrasting against his stubble-covered jaw.

Suddenly overcome with pure lust, Charlotte found her arms wrapping around his neck, and he responded quickly, grabbing her lower back and thrusting their bodies together. They kissed passionately, arms enveloping each other, giving in to their burning attraction and abandoning all inhibitions. Charlotte played with his thick black hair as his hands slid around her back, shoulders and hips. He squeezed her backside, and she moaned as they continued to kiss, their desire increasing with every passing second.

Suddenly, a loud bang from behind violently broke their bodies apart, and they looked in unison at Meeks, who was leaning against the door.

"Hey, you guys... I'm sorry to interrupt... wow, this is uncomfortable. Ant, I need to warn you: Lucia is right outside at reception, and she's looking for you. Char, honey, you'd better come with me."

Charlotte's hand shot up to her mouth, the other smoothing down her hair and clothes. Her breathing still ragged, she cleared her throat and attempted to straighten herself.

"Meeks, um... I..."

"Honey, don't worry, there's no time. Come with me, now!" He grabbed Charlotte's hand as he rushed past her and headed to the other side of the room. As they approached the back door, she looked back briefly and saw Antonio slapping his face, fastening the top two buttons of his shirt and smoothing his dishevelled hair.

Exhaling audibly, he strode over to the door, opened it and walked out towards the bright reception area.

What the bloody hell just happened?

Meeks and Charlotte made their way through a few darkened corridors, then through a fire exit and out into brilliant sunshine.

"Meeksy, where are we going?" Charlotte asked, surprised by how quickly he was walking.

"As far away from danger as I can get you," he said calmly as they walked towards one of the restaurants in the studio complex. Greeted warmly by the maitre d'hotel, Meeks leaned in and spoke quietly. "Bron, we've been here for the last half hour, and you've overheard us talking about the horror movie franchise. Can you take us to our table *discreetly* please?"

The waiter nodded curtly and took them behind a wall, which, judging by the noise Charlotte could hear, led them to the kitchens. She gave a small smile to the wait staff and chefs, who turned a blind eye to the two customers tramping through their domain at high speed. Going through another doorway, they came out into a beautifully lit room slightly cordoned off with a waist-high wall. Crisp white linen tablecloths and gleaming silver and glassware were set on the tabletop, and bright pink peonies were arranged in silver pots on each table.

Charlotte was ushered to one of the chairs taken out for her by the maitre d'hotel.

"Champagne please, Bron."

"Very good."

Meeks laced his hands together and looked at Charlotte. She looked up at him, unsure what he would say next. She could feel her cheeks flush with shame and went to speak.

He held up his hand. "Honey, I don't want you to feel embarrassed, or bad for what just happened. God knows I've seen and done a hundred times worse, believe me. However, I don't need to tell you that this could all backfire, badly."

Charlotte looked down and fiddled with her napkin. "I know, and I'm sorry."

"Char, look at me, there's no need to be sorry! It's just of all the people, that's probably not the one you want to be caught with your pants down... so to speak."

Charlotte snorted and thanked Bron as he poured her a glass of champagne. She drank some and felt her eyes water as the bubbles fizzed in her mouth.

"I would love to see you and Antonio together... you are such a sweet, adorable couple, and he has been miserable for so long. I have to say I've seen such a transformation in him since you came into our lives, Charlotte. He talks about you all the time. We just need to be careful though because we're surrounded by snakes. Snakes that can harm you. I'm saying all this because, well, you may have noticed, I'm kinda fond of you, kid."

Charlotte smiled, feeling emotion stirring in her heart. It was so nice to feel protected in Kev's absence, especially by an older male figure. She smiled lovingly, then leaned forward on the table, head in her hands.

"Meeksy, it's such a mess. What the hell am I doing? I'm dating a movie star and I'm in love with a director. No idea what I'm doing, just a country girl from Australia. A goofy, accident-prone bogan from butt-frack nowhere. I'm messy and unsophisticated and always say the wrong thing. What do these guys even see in me? I just don't belong here."

Meeks reached across the table and grabbed her hand. "Because you're real. You're beautiful, humble and charming. You make all the shellacked nails, fake eyelashes, cheesy veneers and big hair look hollow and cheap. You're true-blue, Char; you're authentic in a sea of fakers. That's what we love about you. And that's what the 99% of insecure people here want to destroy."

Charlotte felt tears brimming in her eyes, embarrassed by this unbidden emotion.

"What would I do without you?" she asked, holding his hand tight.

"Probably struggle with ordering coffees, I'd say."

Charlotte cackled with laughter, causing several nearby diners to turn and stare. She blew her nose loudly on a tissue she found in her pocket. Looking up again, she felt her heart stop; Antonio was across the room, approaching their table, his expression unreadable. Reaching for her glass, she felt her hand tremble as she attempted to take a sip. Behind Antonio, she saw a short, tanned and angry-looking woman... Lucia.

Charlotte glared at Meeks as the colour drained from her face.

"Ahh, hey, folks! You joining us for lunch? Brian and Jake are on their way, we've just been hanging out, talkin' post-production."

Lucia was clutching a bag with the *Hermes* label on it, and while her mouth smiled, her green eyes looked menacing. Antonio was looking intently at Meeks as he pulled out a chair, as if actively to avoid eye contact with Charlotte.

"Lucia, I don't think you've met our new make-up artist protégé, Charlotte Grant from Australia," Meeks said amiably as he gestured across the table.

Standing, Lucia glanced at Charlotte dismissively, then sneered at her outstretched hand. She hooked her bag on the edge of a chair, then snapped her manicured fingers in the air. "Polar," she said loudly with a husky Spanish accent, glaring as Bron approached. She remained standing in the way, making Bron move around her awkwardly, just so he could pull her seat out for her. Flicking her long, shiny, dark hair as she sat, she then sighed and looked at Meeks.

"Edward, is this another one of your... how do you say, adopting strays? Why do we share our table with a nobody from a foreign country?"

Charlotte's eyes widened, her jaw dropped.

"Lucia! Don't speak to people like that, please!" Antonio snapped, banging his fist on the table. Lucia, smirking and completely nonplussed, turned to reach into her bag.

"Lucia, are you listening to me? You want to talk about nobodies? What have you ever accomplished, apart from stealing people's money? Apologise to Charlotte right now! She is ten-times the woman that you are."

Charlotte, holding her breath, looked across at Meeks in disbelief, who closed his eyes and pressed his face into his hand.

Oh, no.

Lucia looked up from her phone. "*What did you just say to me?*"

Antonio stood and leaned over the table, glaring at Lucia; Charlotte could see his arm muscles trembling ever so slightly.

"I said, she is *ten-times the woman you are.* The only thing you're good at is stealing other people's money!"

At that moment, the situation went haywire; Bron, arriving with Lucia's sparkling water, stepped back, as if well-practiced; a heated exchange in Spanish occurred across the table between Lucia and Antonio; Meeks rose from his chair and walked calmly over to a gaping Charlotte, ushering her out of the same door they had come in. As they hurried down the corridor, he turned back to speak to her.

"Honey, I never thought I'd say this, but I'm taking you back to somewhere less hostile."

"Where's that?"

"To Amanda!"

CHAPTER 11

Charlotte could feel her heart drumming in her ears, while her hands continued to tremble with the sudden turn of events at lunch. Meeks had taken Charlotte back to the make-up-artistry HQ building via a cafe that sold delicious-looking sandwiches. So much had happened in such a short time; there was much for her to process while keeping a cool head and returning to work.

"Here, Char, eat this," said Meeks, handing her a paper bag. "I got you a couple of 'sangers' as you would say, plus coffees to take back to Tess and Amanda. It'll be a hard afternoon, but anything is better than listening to those two going at it. Trust me."

Surprised by how much the last hour had rattled her, Charlotte looked at Meeks quizzically. "Matey, I don't understand. They're separated, yeah? Why was she even here? Like, why not just divorce her and get it over with? Why spend time with someone you hate that much?"

His lips tightened and he nodded. "I don't like to talk smack about anyone, but Lucia... now there's a piece of work. She has the best lawyers money can buy, who've somehow managed to ensure she's secured a substantial portion of Antonio's studio and all his investments. As well as their little girls, who sadly she uses as emotional leverage over Antonio. Lucia manages to stay involved in just about everything he does."

Charlotte threw up her hands in frustration. "Oh my God! That is... that's disgusting. I knew it was bad, but... can't he just buy her out? Like, surely having less money would be worth getting rid of her?"

"Believe me, Ant has confided in me many times that he'd be happy to give her every penny he owns and have nothing, just custody of the kids. But Lucia won't budge. She doesn't even spend much time with the girls. I've seen her, it's horrific to watch her 'mothering skills,' or lack thereof. Seeing Antonio suffer and having control over him... not allowing him to move on and be happy with someone else... gives her immense pleasure."

Charlotte shook her head in disbelief. Meeks' expression changed, and he looked at her earnestly. "Luckily, I've seen a change in him recently. Antonio is finally standing up to her, like we just witnessed; that wouldn't have happened six months ago. As his friend, it's great to see, kiddo, let me tell you. Honestly, I think he's found someone worth fighting for." Meeks smiled.

Holy effing shit. This is HUGE. Why did I go to the bar that night? I could have avoided all this trouble. Why? Why didn't I just go home? Goddammit, Charlotte Grant, I KNEW this would happen.

As if reading her thoughts, Meeks took the lunch bag she was holding and placed them on the nearby bench.

"Charlotte, none of this is your fault. I could see the sparks flying between you two from day one. It's okay, these things happen! But I want to make sure you're protected. This is why I want you to consider some of the project offerings I've mentioned."

Charlotte's nose wrinkled. "But I'm straight off the boat. I have virtually no experience, and I can't act for shit."

"I'll teach you the ropes, it's okay, I've got you. Plus, if any of this stuff with Ant blows up and you're working for me, it'll ensure Amanda can't touch you."

Charlotte took a deep breath. "Okay, I hear what you're saying. And thank you, dear friend. Give me a couple of days, okay? I just need a couple of days to get my head straight. Work and everything are so insane, I just have no brain space to think about anything. The last thing I want to do is rush into something, then let you down. I want to make you proud. Is that okay?"

He smiled and patted her arm. "Of course it is, honey. I understand. And I'm certain you won't let me down. But we're moving pretty quickly on this one, so we'll need your decision soon. Okay?"

Charlotte nodded enthusiastically as he continued. "Just one other thing... little piece of advice."

"Yeah?"

"If you're going on another date with Liam Reeves, maybe... best not to tell Antonio. Liam slept with Lucia; it was the final straw in their marriage collapse."

Charlotte gasped.

"He *what?*"

"Yeah. That's why Antonio hates him. Liam is a playboy, and although he's dreamy, he's really not worth getting in trouble for.

I'd steer clear of that one, baby girl. Ant's life is a total shit-show right now, but at least he's a nice guy, and you can trust him. Plus, he told me he's in love with you... so that's a factor to consider."

Charlotte felt her head implode for what felt like the fiftieth time today.

He's actually in love with me. Antonio Sanchez is in love... with ME.

She couldn't quite believe it, but she was actually looking forward to going back to work, just to escape from all this overwhelming information.

"Nice of you to drop by," Amanda drawled as Charlotte walked into the make-up art room, juggling food, the tray of coffees and her belongings.

She beamed at Amanda. "Hey, boss! I brought you both some snacks!" Charlotte replied cheerfully. She gave Tess a peck on the cheek as she delivered her lunch.

"Skinny mocha, hot, no foam. That's your coffee, right boss?" She handed the coffee to Amanda, who looked at it, then at Charlotte, as if conflicted by the urge to yell and express some kind of gratitude.

Charlotte decided to carry on talking, regardless, especially when she saw the mask Tess had been working on. "Tess, oh my gosh, girl, that looks amazing! That prosthetic is for the retake of the final battle scene, yeah?"

"Thanks, girl! Yeah, it is. Do you think the blood over this side looks okay, like too dried or needs to be fresher? The muscle tissue might need to be whiter, I dunno."

They stood back and admired the mask.

Amanda, looking like all the wind had been taken out of her

sails, looked at her coffee, then the mask, then left the room. Charlotte and Tess looked at each other surreptitiously.

"Well, *that* went better than I thought it would," she whispered through clenched teeth.

"Agreed! So, what happened? How'd it go?"

Charlotte put her hands on her hips and shook her head. "I don't even know where to freakin' start. Let's go find somewhere quiet and I'll tell you the story while we scoff these down."

By the time Charlotte finished telling her story, and Tess had gasped enough times to validate the fear picking away at her brain, confirming this *was* in fact a huge deal, that she was definitely *not* overreacting, she had only taken one bite of her sandwich.

Despite all her efforts, Charlotte had managed to throw herself into a maelstrom of disaster. Furthermore, she needed to respond to Meeks shortly with her answer about whether she wanted to make the career switch. There were just too many distractions; working insane hours, men, crazy bitches and underlying homesickness were constant stressors.

Should she switch jobs? What if it didn't work out, and she let Meeks down and disappointed everyone? Could Meeks and she still be friends, with him as her new manager? What about her work visa? She would need to apply for a new one under a different company's sponsorship... What would happen to Tess if she just up and left?

Her inability to talk through her decisions properly was also starting to bother her. She missed those times at the pub where she'd get everyone's opinion, weigh it up, then make her choice. Tess was the only one here she could talk to. But there was never enough time to tell Tess everything that was happening. She'd get through the headlines, only to be interrupted before the climax. Charlotte felt bad about contacting Tess after hours to talk about her predicament; she already gave her so much, and as it stood, Tess barely had any time to spend with her kids.

What I wouldn't give to be teleported back home, even just for a night, so I could have a decent yarn with Kev and Mave.

Before she could explore the thought, Charlotte felt something flick her backside. Swinging around to see who or what it was, she found Liam standing there, arms folded, wearing a smug smile. Charlotte gasped and looked around to see if Amanda was nearby.

"Liam! What are you doing, my boss could be watching you?"

He shrugged. "I do that to everyone, not only the hot chicks I've dated."

"Well, there will be one less hot chick around if my boss sees you touching my bum...."

"So what? We'll get you another job in a heartbeat." With that, he grabbed Charlotte, pulled her in and kissed her on the mouth.

She struggled and finally managed to push him away. Gasping with shock, she slapped him across the cheek.

"What the... no!" Charlotte said, flailing her arms in disbelief.

Liam simply laughed and sauntered off towards the catering table, doing some finger guns to a guy, presumably a friend of his, as he arrived. Swivelling back to the mask she was working on, Charlotte's heart almost stopped when she saw her... Amanda... eyes locked and jaw set. It was like watching a juggernaut coming towards her, gaining speed and ferocity with every step.

This is it. I'm dead. Or fired. Or dead and fired. It's over. Panic.

And in an instant, Charlotte's intuition took over.

It's okay, I've got this.

Looking at the floor, Charlotte felt tears well in her eyes, which, given the events of the morning, weren't so difficult to procure.

One hand on her heart, the other over her mouth, she started to breathe heavily, as if her airway was restricted. She looked at the floor with tears streaming down her face. Looking up at Amanda, now right in front of her, Charlotte said, "I don't know... I don't know why he did that. I didn't even..."

Through her tears, Charlotte could almost see the cogs turning in her boss's head.

"I don't know what you're playing at, Charlotte, or what this is. But if I ever, EVER see you with Liam Reeves again, that's it. You're done. You're not allowed to work on him from this point onwards. Got it?"

Charlotte nodded, a little taken aback by her reaction, as she expected to be fired on the spot. She watched as Amanda stormed off, leaving a bewildered Charlotte in her wake.

Wait, if I had genuinely been upset, and that was blatant sexual abuse, not only is Amanda okay with that, but she's blaming ME? What the actual...?

As Charlotte processed this sobering information, and wiped her eyes and face, Tess ran up to her.

"Oh, honey, what is it? Are you okay? I had to go check in with the wardrobe team. What happened?"

"Liam Reeves, that's what happened... that jerk actually *kissed* me, Tess. Kissed me right here, in front of everyone. No asking, just did it. Amanda saw it and yelled at *ME, even though she saw me slap him.*"

Tess shook her head. "Yeah, that doesn't surprise me. It horrifies me but doesn't surprise me."

Charlotte turned to her friend. "Tess, I think I'm done. I don't think I can take this anymore. All the insults and the lack of encouragement. Yeah, it's tough... but this... that was just disgusting."

Silence hung between them, with Tess gently stroking Charlotte's arm.

"Girl, I get it. Let's just say, *I get it.* Sexual harassment is rife in our industry. And some days, if I didn't have my babies to feed, I would have smacked that bitch's ass to Friday. Don't even get me started on those sexist pigs like Liam who think it's funny to behave like that. It's not okay."

Charlotte nodded, still numb and unable to comment; her brain was experiencing information overload.

"Okay, this is the plan. You got all them offers from Meeks, with all those other projects. Next week, they're all away; every boss in the studio will be on the other side of the country. The rest of our make-up team will be back, it'll be fun! Plus, you got Disneyland tomorrow." She elbowed Charlotte suggestively.

Charlotte smiled, sniffed, and looked at her friend's smiling face.

A week. I'll give it a week. For Tess. In the meantime, I might call Meeks for more details on those offers.

CHAPTER 12

Charlotte awoke with a start. Narrow slivers of light stretched across the ceiling from the window blind left slightly open the night before. Her mind had been so preoccupied with the unfolding drama surrounding her that both her dreams and work life had melded into one continuous loop.

Today was different though; after many years of dreaming about it, she was finally going to Disneyland.

She leapt out of bed, walked over to roll up the blinds and looked out at the morning skyline. Another beautiful, sunny day in LA.

As per their arrangement, Antonio's limo would be pulling up outside around 7am. Rather than the regular nervousness Charlotte had felt in the pit of her stomach over the last few weeks, amplified over the last few days by recent events, she was genuinely really excited about today. She ate a quick breakfast, dressed in a t-shirt, jeans and trainers, with a simple hair style and minimal makeup. If

Antonio felt as strongly about her as she did about him, how she looked wouldn't matter. Besides, she'd likely be getting messy with the girls, would no doubt spill something over herself, and had no intention whatsoever of trying to keep clean and act like a grown up.

Charlotte filled her water bottle and replenished a few other items in her backpack, but then became distracted by a new text message:

Hi Charlotte. We are downstairs. Get ready for questions about Koala bears. Take your time. A x

The butterflies in her stomach so far kept under wraps this morning suddenly exploded. The excitement of going to Disneyland and her newfound love for Antonio were too much to handle.

Cool. Keep it cool, Grant. You are walking into a potential shitstorm. Just keep it in your pants. Even if you're crazy about each other, this isn't going to work. And if he doesn't put a stop to all this, you need to. Now, KNOCK IT OFF.

"Auntie Charlotte!" Bella and Olivia shouted in unison, their two little, happy faces peering out of the limousine window.

Charlotte closed the front door behind her and waved enthusiastically from the top of the steps. Running towards them, the scenery around her suddenly blurred and went dark for a moment. Charlotte realised she was now lying on the ground with her cheek on something cold and sticky. There was a flurry of activity around her, and as she rolled onto her back, she saw four concerned faces looking at her.

"Uugghhhh…" she moaned.

"Charlotte, dearest, you alright? Have you hit your head? Can you see me? Say something." Concern was etched on Antonio's upside-down face and was evident in the urgency of his tone.

"Something," she slurred.

"Mr Sanchez, should I call for an ambulance?" Hugo asked, also sounding concerned.

"What... what? What is that on my face? Shit! Did my brain fall out? Fark!" Charlotte clawed at her cheek, feeling something foreign stuck there.

"Darling, no... you tripped and landed on a bag of garbage. You've got chewing gum stuck to your cheek. Don't worry, your beautiful face is still intact."

Charlotte looked at him, then at the dirty, stringy strand of gum she had just peeled off her face. She looked around, feeling the panic subside, and laughed.

The two girls looked at each other, then at their father. Then they saw the funny side, too, and laughed along with Charlotte at her expense.

Before long, they were all laughing hysterically, Charlotte loudest of all. Hugo seemed to be the least amused and had gone to fetch a pack of antiseptic wipes from the limousine. He and Antonio helped her sit upright and extract the remnants of the gum left on her face.

Olivia spoke first, pointing at Charlotte's feet. "Auntie Char, your shoe is untied."

"Well spotted, little bean. It's because I have two left feet, you see. They don't make laces for people like me."

Olivia looked at her quizzically, then gave a shy smile when she got the joke.

"Are you okay to get up?" Antonio asked. "Do you need a sip of water first?"

Hugo, anticipating the offer, leaned over holding a bottle of water he'd just opened.

"Thank you, Hugo," she said, taking a swig.

Antonio swept the hair off her face and looked at her adoringly.

"I'm okay, just a total un-co," Charlotte said quietly, gazing back at him.

"A what?"

"Never mind. Okay, let's go," she said, hoisting herself up with the help of the two men.

Antonio kept one hand on her back as she steadied herself while the other held her hand.

Hugo had rushed ahead to get the door and leaned across the top with his arm.

Bless him, he's protecting me from hitting my head... again. What a lovely man.

"Thank you, Hugo, you're a sweetheart." She made her way slowly to the limousine.

He looked down at his polished shoes, his cheeks flushed and muttered something about it being no bother.

Bella handed Charlotte's bag to Antonio, and they all made their way into the limo unscathed.

Charlotte's pride had been hurt a little, along with a slight graze along her cheekbone. She joked with the family that at least her face was now balanced; an egg on her forehead on one side, a scratched cheekbone on the other. Along with periodic checks on her well-being, the forty-minute ride was spent talking about Australia, with the girls peppering Charlotte with questions about its native animals.

"Well, first off, in Australia, we abbreviate people's names a lot, so you would be Liv, and you would be Bels... your daddy would probably be Tones, or Sancho. So, Liv, to answer your earlier question, number six hundred and fifty-three, Koalas aren't actually *bears*. Even though they're cute and fuzzy like a bear. It's kinda weird because we're all upside down over there." Before she could elaborate on the joke, they turned off the freeway and she saw the Disneyland castle towering majestically over the treetops.

Holy, effing, crap-balls.

The limo slowed, and the girls pressed their faces up against the glass, straining for a better look. Charlotte saw Hugo get out once they'd stopped, making his way around to their door.

Antonio got out first and helped the girls out, then Charlotte by taking her hand. She stood close to him, and they shared a moment together. Her head was swimming again, and not due to her latest injury.

"You are so good with my children... you're a natural," he said, and she felt his minty breath on her cheek.

"They're so easy to get along with, it's a breeze! Oh, hey look, there's virtually no line! You beauty!"

Antonio smiled with a slightly awkward expression. "Oh, it's okay, Char... we don't need to line up. The passes we have are VIP, so no waiting required."

Slightly embarrassed, she said, "Oh, okay. Cool!"

Of course, they were rich and probably did their weekly food shop in the bloody limo. Wait, they wouldn't do their own shopping. Let alone in a limousine. Why would they need to?

She waved goodbye to Hugo, who first looked surprised, then reciprocated before sliding into the driver's seat.

I wonder what Hugo's doing now. Should we have invited him to come with us? Man, being rich is bloody complicated.

She pushed these and other thoughts from her mind as she walked through the gates and approached the main entrance. Everything was big, beautiful, colourful and looked almost edible. Mickey and Minnie Mouse greeted the early morning visitors with enthusiastic waves, their fixed expressions of happiness mirroring Charlotte's. She felt like she'd regressed in age by a couple of decades.

"Arrrghhh! I'm in Disneyland!" she squealed, jumping up and down. The girls, infected with the same excitement, joined her, and before long, the four of them were holding hands and bouncing on the spot. Their joy soon spread to the mascots, who also started jumping alongside them.

Okay this is already the best day of my life. There are giant mice, and everything looks like it's made from lollies.

"Alright, team, where do we want to go first?" Antonio asked, studying one of the maps they'd been given by the ticket booth assistant. "Magic mountain? Roller coasters? Teacup rides?"

"Teacup ride!" yelled Bella.

"Roller coasters!" yelled Olivia.

"EVERYTHING!" yelled Charlotte.

Antonio laughed.

"Okay, Bella my darling, you got in first, so let's start off gently and go get in a giant teacup. Last one there's a rotten egg!" He ran off, slowly so the girls could easily run after him.

Charlotte's heart exploded with love once more.

The teacups had been surprisingly fun for Charlotte, who thought they might be better suited to little kids. She had been on every ride at Luna Park after she'd done her make-up art exam in Sydney. The higher, faster and scarier, the better. But watching how much the girls enjoyed themselves was just as much fun as screaming her guts out.

The atmosphere between her and Antonio had been more pleasant than she'd expected, considering the tumultuous week that had just passed. It warmed Charlotte's heart to see how happy and carefree he looked. There was always a tension, a worry on that tanned brow, which seemed to constantly weigh him down, but not today. If it were possible, he looked even more handsome. And he seemed like such a good father, the way he'd take time and explain things. Even when it came to discipline, he seemed to get the balance right.

Today, we're in a bubble. Today we don't worry about anything, we just have fun.

"Papa, can I please talk to you about something?" Bella asked as they stopped by a gift shop.

"Of course, my love, what is it?"

Bella whispered in her father's ear, glancing at Charlotte from behind her cupped little hand.

Antonio stood, nodded and patted his youngest on the head. He stepped forward and his face grew serious for a moment.

"Charlotte, it has been requested that you please stand over there, outside for a moment. There are things that... need to be purchased, secret things, without you looking."

Charlotte laughed, then tapped the side of her nose. "Got it. I'll be out the front, chatting to Ariel about princess stuff." Suddenly, he leaned in and kissed her on her grazed cheek, ever so gently. She felt her legs weaken.

"Thank you," he said, breathing deeply.

"Mehhghughh," she mumbled, floating in the direction of the outside racks of sunglasses and stuffed toys. She sighed happily and absorbed the colours and textures surrounding her. The softness of the plush merchandise, the grey cobbled stone streets. The bright sunlight that bounced off the canvas umbrellas, the differing colours denoting the various eating establishments. Cream coloured buildings with bright signs of differing shapes.

Princess Elsa stood a little ways in front of her in a sparkling blue hooped dress, impeccably braided golden hair piled on top of her head, with stage-show makeup on.

I wonder how she goes all day with that lot trowelled on.

Charlotte jumped when something grabbed her leg. She looked down, and Bella was holding something small and grey in her little closed hands, smiling broadly. Olivia stood next to her, looking up at Charlotte.

"Auntie Char, Liv and I wanted to get you something. It's a little rabbit. You said before you didn't have a rabbit to blame when you jumped in puddles. Now you have Poncho junior, so if he makes trouble, you can blame him. And they're rabbit brothers, so even if you go back to Australia, you can remember us."

Charlotte brought her fingers up to her trembling lips. Tears filled her eyes and leaked down her cheeks as she blinked. Crouching down to take Poncho Junior from Bella, she reached out to grab the little girls and squeezed them tight.

"I *love* him. Girls, this is seriously the best present I've ever got. *Ever*. Thank you." She sobbed and laughed simultaneously.

The girls beamed at their father, then ran off to look at a bubble machine nearby that had just started up. Charlotte knelt, found a packet of tissues in her bag and blew her nose. When she stood, Antonio took her into his arms, and she felt more loved, more accepted for who she was than she had in a long time. Kev and Mave were like the blood-relatives she'd wished she'd had, but this was different. This felt like the beginnings of love with her *own* family.

The foursome watched the sunset from a lovely little bar near the front entrance, which only VIP-pass holders could access. Antonio had asked Charlotte if she was a fan of champagne, then proceeded to get the most expensive bottle on the menu. The girls ordered milkshakes, and Charlotte could tell they were becoming sleepy.

I bet those little tykes will be sleeping home in the car. Geezo, they are so easily pleased. It's like they're just desperately starved for affection; it's heartbreaking.

They chatted happily about the most amazing, wonderful, fun-filled day imaginable. Charlotte had gone on just about every ride, some with the girls, some without.

Antonio asked a couple of times whether she could look after the girls while he went on a ride or two. The height restriction wouldn't allow Bella and Olivia, however much they pleaded.

They had bought way too much merchandise to take home with them, and Antonio had won an oversized panda at a shooting game, which he gave to Charlotte. Cotton candy, ice-cream and hot dogs were consumed along with a variety of other junk foods.

As they sipped their drinks, the streetlights were switched on, and the Disneyland attendees let out a chorus of "ooo's" and "ahh's."

Antonio checked his phone that until this point had been switched off. "Ahh, guys, Hugo is outside. We'll need to finish up and go meet him! Got everything we need? You have Poncho Senior?"

Bella produced Poncho from her bag and nodded. "Poncho Junior?"

Charlotte copied the action with her own stuffed rabbit.

Walking out into the warm twilight air, Charlotte offered to take Bella on a piggy-back ride and hold Olivia's hand while Antonio had to make some urgent calls. She looked back when she heard him raise his voice and sadly saw that wonderful carefree look on his face disappear. Whomever he was talking to, they brought him crashing back to reality with powerful aftershocks.

Money doesn't buy happiness. I knew that before I came here, but now I see it's true.

Desperate to help Antonio or at least comfort him, Charlotte figured the best way to assist would be to entertain the girls and make sure they were looked after. As they ducked through the ticket entrance, they caught a glimpse of Hugo beside the limo. Charlotte crouched so Bella could slide off her back, then grabbed their bags and souvenirs.

"Warm greetings, Miss Grant," said Hugo. "Did you have fun today?"

"Hugo!! Oh my goodness, did we ever," she said, beaming and puffing from all the exertion. "It was the best, just the best. I don't think I'll ever forget it.",

He smiled and took their belongings, placing them in the boot.

Charlotte refrained this time from opening her own door and held the hands of the girls instead. They all climbed into the roomy limo, and Charlotte shuffled over so Antonio could slide in easily once off the phone.

"He's probably talking to Mama," Olivia said sadly as she crossed her legs on the seat opposite, clicking in her own seatbelt and her little sister's.

"They fight a lot, eh, Liv?" Charlotte asked quietly.

Olivia nodded.

"All the time. Mama is mean. She's mean to Papa, and she's mean to us. When we see her... we don't see her very much though, it's normally our nanny. She's nice. Not as nice as you, though."

Charlotte smiled sadly, feeling her heart breaking. These poor little girls just wanted love and attention... exactly the same things she'd wanted when she was a little girl being ignored. They weren't entitled little shits like many of the rich kids Charlotte had encountered at work and around town. These two girls had been raised well, despite their mother's negative influence.

It's none of my business, I should just keep out of it.

Charlotte could see Antonio leaning against the edge of the limo. His phone was peeking out the top of his jeans' pocket, so he wasn't on it anymore. He stood back and she could see his chest rise and fall deeply. He then got in the limo with a smile that had just been slapped on.

"We're good to go, thank you, Hugo," Antonio said as he closed the limo door behind him. "You okay, girls? Seatbelts on?"

Charlotte could already see their little eyes looking heavy, and Bella was resting her head on Poncho.

Antonio took another deep breath, and without looking at her, reached over the seat to hold Charlotte's hand.

She didn't look either; just squeezed to let him know she was okay with it, as they watched the twinkling lights of L.A. zip past on their way home.

As they pulled up outside Charlotte's apartment, she quietly said goodbye to the dozing little girls. Antonio leaned in and kissed them both on the head and told them he was going to see Auntie Charlotte to her door. They stirred, mumbled their goodbyes and then drifted back to sleep.

"Thank you, Hugo, and thanks just for being an awesome dude in general," Charlotte said as she took her belongings from their driver.

He nodded and gave a little bow before standing solemnly by the limo.

Antonio walked up behind her, standing very close after they reached the top step.

"Thank you so much for coming with us today. You are my sunshine, Charlotte." He held one of her hands and the other across his chest. "You have no idea what it means to me. You have no idea what *you* mean to me." Their eyes burned together for a moment, and Charlotte felt the need to speak first.

"Ant... this is really tough. You're going through a lot. Your kids are *awesome*. But I'm just a make-up artist. This all feels really big, and like my involvement with you would just make things more complicated. I feel like I've already made it worse. If my boss finds out how I feel about you, I'm toast. If your wife finds out about how I feel about you, I'm toast. Either way, I'm toast. I just think maybe... we should cool it off, and I should get past my last few months. Then we can see." She looked down at the ground. "I dunno."

As she spoke, she felt more like a brick was slowly falling from her chest. She was in love with this man but had to be honest with herself and about the situation. Them getting together and taking this new relationship any further at this point in time was a terrible idea.

Antonio took a step back, as if her words had stung him. His expression changed from looking hurt, then thoughtful, then resigned. He nodded, then sighed deeply as he put his hands on his hips. "You're probably right, Charlotte. It's very mature of you. I want us to be together... at least try. Can you please think about leaving Amanda and coming to work with Meeks and me? That could make things easier for us?"

Charlotte pouted. "It *could* make things easier... or it could backfire, badly. I think that for now, we should just be friends. Is that okay?"

He looked at her with those dark, smouldering eyes, and Charlotte couldn't tell whether he was about to cry. She desperately hoped not.

"You are the best thing that's ever come into my life, Charlotte. I'm not going to give you up without a fight. I'll be friends, if that's what you want. But know that I want... that I want so much more than that. I want you."

Charlotte gulped audibly.

This is the part where you leave, Charlotte, before your weakened resolve turns into complete mush.

"Okay. I love, um, thank you, Ant. I just had the best day." Before he could respond and change her mind, she whipped her keys out to unlock the door and rushed inside. Having closed the door, she rushed up the stairs carrying multiple bags of Disney merchandise.

Okay, what just happened. Did I do the right thing? I don't know... did I? Crap, shit, crap bollocks.

Her phone buzzed with a text message. She took her phone out of her bag and unlocked the screen:

Charlotte... my love. I miss you already.

You are so right about our situation, and you are right to keep things as friendship. We Spanish men are not known for our abstinence or our control. If I had my way, things would be... well, let's just say we would be in the same room together right now... and not this far apart.

My parents would like to meet you. We are having a party next Friday night after I get back from New York City. Can you please come? I would love you to be there.

I would love you to be anywhere, as long as it's with me.
A x"

Charlotte must have read the message at least fifty times during the night. She fell asleep with her phone in her hand, imagining an alternate timeline where they could be together and happy in love.

CHAPTER 13

The week wore on smoothly and without incident with all the site managers, directors and executives away in New York City. It made for a pleasant week. All make-up artists were back on board, having returned from working on other locations around the country. Charlotte found the banter between the reunited team fun and energising. Jokes about Amanda were rife, and although everyone seemed less stressed and a lot more pleasant—Zephyr actually praised Charlotte on a prosthetic arm she'd done—they were still productive.

However, Charlotte had a current problem of a different nature; she was sweating, and it didn't bode well for her evening plans.

It was Friday afternoon and somehow, she'd have to find a way to change at the off-site set, have a shower and change into the clothes she'd shoved into her backpack.

Then, wearing heels and possibly riding a pushbike to a dinner party with Antonio's entire family for the first time, she would have to ensure she remained calm and collected in front of that cow of a wife, Lucia, whom she strongly suspected would be there.

It's all okay. We cleared out Trev's ute with that nest of huntsman spiders. I can make this work.

Cleaned up and changed, Charlotte winced as her bare feet made contact with the cold, jagged pedals and pushed off in the direction of the door. The helmet she'd found nearby had either bloodstains or ketchup on the side and squeezed her head a little harder than she cared for.

Apart from the staring and cars honking their horns, Charlotte's twenty-minute bike ride was thankfully uneventful, but her dishevelled state when she arrived at the address Antonio gave her had her concerned. She stopped outside the most gargantuan gates on a road full of gargantuan gates. She could tell it was Antonio's family by the age and authenticity, quite different from the new McMansions that lined the wide street.

A guard looked her up and down. "Uhh... can I help you, Miss?"

Charlotte was still puffing from the frantic cycle, her cheeks flushed and her hair a windswept mess. She dreaded to think what her makeup looked like.

"Hi! I'm... here... to... see... Antonio! And the family—the dinner thing."

"Uh... you are on the guest list for tonight?"

Charlotte nodded enthusiastically and held the stitch in her right side.

The guard grabbed the walkie-talkie from his belt and spoke Spanish into it; Charlotte was certain he was using an interesting way to describe her, especially when he used the word 'loco.' He nodded and replaced the walkie-talkie.

"Mr Sanchez has asked you to please come straight in. You can park your uh... vehicle out the front, Miss." He looked at the bike with disdain.

"No valet parking? What kind of place is this!?" Charlotte feigned outrage in between puffs. "Do you know how much this bike is *worth*?" She wiggled the bike's flagpole on the back. She couldn't tell whether the guard's look was more shock or confusion. "Don't worry mate I'm just joshin' ya. You're all good. See ya!" She waved goodbye, then wobbled and kicked off again up the driveway, uncertain how much longer she'd have to pedal as the road twisted and turned, with the manicured gardens and trees obscuring the way ahead.

What seemed like an eternity later, a huge Spanish-style estate came into view. Charlotte looked up and gasped; the whitewash façade, ironwork, red tile roof and ochre tubs full of blooming geraniums were all like something from a magazine cover. Antonio hadn't mentioned explicitly that his family was wealthy, and his humility wouldn't indicate he came from money. Charlotte had encountered a lot of rich people during her time in Hollywood, and Antonio certainly didn't act like one of them. She heard him laughing before she saw him hurrying down the steps and out in the late-afternoon sunshine towards her.

"Char... what are you... why?"

Charlotte ungraciously leapt off the bike and shoved her helmet into his hands.

"Shoosh! Here, hold this!" She took off her backpack and fluffed out her green halter-neck top, hoping it would dry quickly. Rifling around in her bag, she found one high heel and then the other. Tottering on one as her toe found the matching shoe on the ground, she grabbed Antonio's outstretched arm until they were fitted.

"Charlotte, seriously, you can't ride a bicycle in L.A. You'll get mugged or killed. *No one* rides a bike here unless they're a courier or a psychopath. Char, next time just call Hugo. That man loves you; he'd drive you to Seattle if you asked him to.", He tried to catch Charlotte's eye as she made adjustments to her skinny black jeans and smoothed down her wild, windswept hair. "Charlotte Grant, are you listening to me?"

"Ready!" she announced, hands outstretched and still slightly out of breath.

Antonio cocked his head and sighed with exasperation. "So stubborn... and yet so breathtakingly beautiful."

Charlotte looked back into his eyes and felt the same electricity between them. She remembered his message from last week, and along with the look he was giving her, she felt a flutter in her heart. A gentle breeze tousled his hair, and she could smell the fragrance he wore; the effect was intoxicating. The sun flickered through the tall trees opposite the front entrance, casting long shadows in amber light; the scene was truly magical. Her breathing settled as she felt herself drawn to him; the all-too familiar feeling of being in love washing over her once again.

Oh my God! I love this man... but you still can't have him, Charlotte.

Charlotte cleared her throat and shook herself out of it. "Shall we go in? I can't wait to meet your fam-bam."

He continued to stare, his eyes burning into hers as he stepped closer and took one of her hands in his. "If anything happened to you... you are my... Charlotte... I..."

"Auntie Char!" Bella and Olivia shouted in unison as they burst through the front doors.

Charlotte blinked and turned towards the excited little girls, welcoming them into her outstretched arms.

"Aww, hello, my little beans!" she said between kisses and hugs. "So good to see you again! How's it going, you good?"

Bella spoke the loudest and waved a colourful piece of paper in her little hand. "I drew a picture of you, Olivia, me and Papa when we went to Disneyland!"

Charlotte took the paper and gasped at it admiringly.

"Bels, look what you did! That's so cool! Who are these little guys?"

"That's me and Liv, of course. I'm a koala and she's a baby jobby."

Charlotte stifled a laugh. "Oh, cool, you mean baby *joey*? Like a teeny tiny kangaroo?" She held her arms up and did a little kangaroo hop.

The girls giggled and hugged Charlotte's leg, jostling each other for prime position.

"Auntie Char! I did a clay model of a koala!" said Olivia with a downturned mouth. "But Papa said I need to keep it on the table until it dries properly."

Charlotte looked up from her crouched position at Antonio, who was looking at her with complete adoration. "That's okay, little joey, let's hop inside and have a look, eh? I want to see this clay masterpiece for myself!" She stood, still facing the girls but feeling that familiar feeling of Antonio's gaze. The girls continued to shout randomly and grab onto Charlotte's hands, pulling her towards the front door.

She grimaced and mouthed 'sorry' as she looked back at Antonio, inclining her head towards the bike and backpack left for him to look after. He had a dazed, smiling face as she turned forward to approach the stone steps.

As Olivia attempted to push open the massive oak door, it was assisted on the other side by a man in uniform, who smiled and nodded as they stepped inside. She admired the plush paisley carpet, dark wood staircase sweeping up with deep red walls adorned with old pictures, their frames ornate and unique. A smell of polished wood, barbequed meat and freshly baked bread wafted tantalisingly through the air.

Ahead, she could see people through a doorway in white uniforms in what Charlotte suspected was the kitchen, and to the left were big open double doors emitting loud chatter, laughter and clinking glasses. Almost instantly, despite this opulence she had never experienced, it felt like a real home to Charlotte. She felt a tear prickle her eye.

I've never felt like I belong anywhere... or to a family... and holy shit, these guys are RICH.

The little girls continued to drag on Charlotte's arm as they made their way through the doors and into the large living room, full of people. An older lady with a kind face looked over in her direction, excused herself from the people she was talking to, put down her drink and hurried over.

"You must be Charlotte! Oh, welcome, my dear, it's wonderful to meet you. I'm Maria, Antonio's mother."

Charlotte smiled warmly; the family resemblance was obvious. "Hello, Maria, it's lovely to meet you. Thank you so much for the invitation, you have the most beautiful home!"

Maria laughed and smoothed down Bella's hair, who was standing closest and still clinging to Charlotte. "My little dears, I am going to look after our important guest and take her on a tour of the house and grounds. Would you like Tata to take you up to the treehouse?"

The little girls protested and clung tighter to Charlotte.

"Tata has cake for you, you can set up for a tea party, okay?"

Bella and Olivia considered the bribe.

"Only if Auntie Char comes to tea, too," said Olivia. "We will set a place for her."

Maria raised her eyebrows and chuckled. "I'm sure that will be fine, if Auntie Char doesn't mind," she said, looking for confirmation.

Charlotte laughed, nodded and looked behind Maria as a large, bearded man approached. "You must be the young lady we've heard so much about," he said, his cheeks a little flushed as he reached for Charlotte's hand and kissed it with a bristly face.

"This is my husband, Carlos," said Maria.

"Pleasure to meet you, sir. Sorry I'm late."

Carlos put a hand over his heart. "Sir? I like this one. She respects her elders." He looked down at his granddaughters. "You take note, little chicas. Now, I overheard talk of a tea party in a treehouse." He crouched and lowered his voice as if planning a conspiracy. "Shall we go together now on horseback?"

The little girls squealed and leapt onto their grandfather's back, causing him to wobble with the weight as he stood back up. Awkwardly they made their way towards the back of the room, and Charlotte watched them happily until she saw a sour face by the open back doors. Lucia. Her eyes were narrowed, heavilyeyeshadowed slits, arms crossed with one bejewelled hand holding a champagne glass.

If looks could kill, I'd be dead on the bloody floor.

Charlotte smiled sweetly at Lucia before turning back to Maria, who seemed to have noted the reaction.

"Ahh, yes. That woman is here, too. She hates being here; the feeling is mutual. I don't know why she comes, but it is what it is."

Instinctively, Charlotte brushed Maria's arm consolingly, facing away from Lucia.

"Does she ever smile?" Charlotte asked with gritted teeth. "I don't think I've ever seen it."

Maria raised her eyebrows in exasperation. "Maybe she'll smile when she gets her hands on Antonio's money. That's the only reason she lowers herself to be around us and her babies. We are looking forward to this chapter being over, believe me."

"I'm sorry to hear that. I hope it'll be over soon."

Maria grinned and took Charlotte's hands in hers. "We have heard so much about you, my dear. Our Antonio is so much happier now with you in his life. The look on his face when he talks about you... his *sunshine*."

Charlotte felt her cheeks blush and an unbidden glaze wash over her eyes. "He's so lovely. And funny. And just... awesome. Back in Australia, we'd call him a 'dag!'"

Maria chuckled and wrinkled her brow. "A... dag?" she asked, still holding Charlotte's hands.

Before Charlotte could explain, she was interrupted by an abrasive voice.

"Maria, I need to talk to Antonio, where is he? My children are now obsessed with Australia, a country founded by filthy criminals.

I'm sick of being the only one to parent these girls. Please tell me where he is!" Lucia completely ignored Charlotte.

Maria's face dropped. She took a deep, steadying breath and squeezed Charlotte's hand tightly before replying.

"Criminals, you say? My grandfather was a criminal, too. He stole bread and meat for his family so we wouldn't starve and was paid a slave's wage. Before he immigrated to America and built all this for us to enjoy. Would you like to speak to his wife, Juana about it? She's sitting right over there." Maria pointed, with forced composure.

Choosing not to look, Lucia raised an eyebrow and pouted. "Guess I'll have to find my *husband* myself then," she sneered, curling her lip at Charlotte and looking her up and down with seeming disgust.

Charlotte blinked with surprise as Lucia stormed towards the front door, then laughed with how absurdly pathetic her behaviour was.

Still holding Charlotte's hand, Maria closed her eyes as she took another deep breath. After a moment she looked up at Charlotte. "My lovely girl, I'm so sorry for that incredible rudeness. It is jealousy. She may be a venomous snake, but Lucia is no fool. She sees Antonio is in love, and she is afraid to lose control. Now more than ever. Please, let's get you a drink and you can meet everyone. We are so happy you're here."

Charlotte found herself instantly forgetting Lucia's spiteful words as the affection for her hosts quickly grew.

Antonio is in love...

CHAPTER 14

A passing waiter was stopped by Maria, who consulted with Charlotte on what she wanted to drink. Still mulling over Maria's comment, it took Charlotte a moment to respond. To make things easier for the waiter, she simply smiled and grabbed a glass of what looked like champagne from the tray he was carrying.

As Maria led her through the room, introducing her to various people, Charlotte could see a range of resembling faces and felt a radiant energy in the room. Families were always a mixed-bag, and she realised just because Antonio was wonderful, it didn't mean all his relations would be. There was an eclectic mix of ages and ethnicities, as well as fashion styles. Two men near the fireplace who looked like they might be twins were dressed in matching red tracksuits. A cooing baby was being held by an older woman by a window. She looked up and smiled at Charlotte as Maria pointed them out. She was employing her 'name game' today, otherwise she'd never remember all these people.

The women made their way through the room and Maria happily introduced Charlotte to anyone available, adding private commentary as to why they were attending. As she followed Maria past the front windows of the room, Charlotte saw movement out on the front circular driveway. She could hear Lucia's screeching before she saw her; arms flailing, red faced, screaming at Antonio. Lucia stepped forward and pushed Antonio, who was hanging onto the handlebars of Charlotte's bike. Rage bubbled inside Charlotte, and she moved quickly to the window, with the room suddenly fading into the background as she witnessed the fight outside.

"My dear, there's nothing we can do," Maria said sadly as she hooked her arm gently around Charlotte's. "It hurts me, too, so much. Antonio's father and I have intervened in so many of their fights, especially when the babies are near; we have found it has done more damage. He needs to stand up to her by himself."

Realising her fists were clenched, Charlotte tried to relax, took a deep breath and squeezed her host's arm.

"It's really bloody difficult, isn't it. Lucia... she just treats him like garbage."

Maria nodded sympathetically, then patted the top of her hand. "Things will work out for the best."

Although they'd only just met, Charlotte felt an instant connection to this woman. They breathed deeply together and laughed at their unplanned synchronicity.

"Shall we continue the tour?" Maria asked brightly, seemingly putting on a brave face.

Led towards the back of the room by her host, they approached a very elderly woman sitting in an ornate yet comfortable-looking wooden chair. Her pale skin stretched over her high cheekbones and a wrinkled mouth, underneath sparse, wiry hairs which sprouted above her lip. Although her deep, brown eyes were sunken, they still sparkled with intelligence. Her gnarled hands curved over the ends of the carved seat like they were part of it.

This must be Juana, Antonio's great grandmother whom Maria mentioned earlier.

Charlotte couldn't help but stare; she was beautiful. Maria turned to Charlotte, who put her drink down on a table, feeling this was an important introduction.

"This is my grandmother, Juana," Maria said with a slightly raised voice. "Bisabuela, this is Charlotte, she is a friend of Antonio's." She then lowered her voice to a whisper. "She speaks a little English, but we suspect she is quite deaf."

Charlotte bowed slightly and smiled at the old lady. "It's lovely to meet you, Madam, and what a beautiful chair that is."

Juana grunted and retracted her hands, wringing them and eyeing the young woman suspiciously.

Charlotte watched Juana's hands as she rubbed them, their movement slow and shaky; protruding knuckles and knotted fingers at awkward angles told a story. She saw the old lady wince in pain and crouched to speak further.

"Juana, are your hands hurting you? Sore? I can massage them if you like? It may help a little." Charlotte made circular motions with her thumbs.

Juana's eyes widened and she looked at Maria, who smiled and addressed her grandmother. "Masaje de manos, Bisabuela? Charlotte puede hacer masajes en las manos."

Juana's shoulders dropped and she looked back to Charlotte hopefully, nodding. "Please. Yes please," Juana croaked.

Charlotte winked at her, then turned to address Maria. "Would I be able to ask for some olive oil from the kitchen, and a couple of little towels Mrs Sanchez? I can grab a chair and do it now, no worries at all. I took a weekend massage course at Sunshine Tafe in Parramatta."

Maria touched her arm and smiled adoringly at her guest. "Please, call me Maria. You are an angel. She is riddled with arthritis, and in much pain. That is so kind of you when you are our guest!" Maria stopped a passing waiter. "Tim, can you please get a little dish, a ramekin of olive oil from the kitchen and some hand towels please?"

Charlotte looked around and found a spare chair near the huge oak table in the middle of the room. Careful not to knock anyone or anything, as was her clumsy custom, she lifted it over to sit on Juana's right side.

"My Nan, uh... my own *bisabuela* had arthritis... very sore."

Juana gave a small nod, still slightly weary of the young woman.

A moment later, the waiter returned with the items.

"Thank you, Timbo," Charlotte said and set a towel underneath Juana's hands to protect the old chair's wood varnish and create a soft resting place. Placing the oil on the small table next to Juana, Charlotte dipped her fingers in the oil and rubbed them together in her own hands before gently picking up Juana's and smoothing it over her age-spotted skin.

Maria stood nearby, quietly speaking to passersby and other family members who had stopped to watch.

Charlotte heard a young woman's voice whisper behind her: "She is brave. I could never do that; Juana would eat me alive."

Charlotte smiled and looked up from her focus; Juana's eyes

showed relief and pleasure. When it was time to switch sides, Charlotte noticed many guests were now looking at what she was doing, and the music seemed louder because the chatter had died down.

Once finished, Charlotte patted the extra oil off and held Juana's hand, giving a small squeeze. "All done, Madam," she said with a kind smile. "Are you feeling okay? Little better?"

Juana looked sleepy, her head resting to one side of the chair's back but with eyes still open. She had a blissful look on her face and leaned forward, placing her hand on Charlotte's cheek. "Thank you. Thank you, hermosa chica."

Charlotte put a hand over hers and again felt the connection, like she'd known these people all her life. "Yay, I'm so glad."

Maria, who'd not gone far during the short treatment, put a hand on Charlotte's shoulder and they regarded each other—her warm smile said it all.

"Bisabuela, would you like to nap now? I can take you to your room?"

Juana was already nodding, seemingly anticipating the question.

Charlotte got up to clear the path and move her chair aside.

Juana smiled sleepily as Maria wheeled her past, the chair apparently equipped with mobility.

"My dear, there is a bathroom down the corridor if you want to wash your hands," said Maria. "I'll be back very soon, and we can continue our tour!"

Charlotte nodded and caught the waiter's eye as he passed, giving him the massage items and thanking him. As she pushed the chair aside further with her hip, she looked up and saw many people smiling at her as they returned to their conversations.

Looking around to find her way to the bathroom, her eyes locked with Antonio's. His smouldering eyes bore into Charlotte's once more. She was immobilised again and kept eye contact as he cut through the crowd towards her.

"Is there anything you can't do?" he asked, shaking his head. "Or anyone you can't charm?"

Charlotte chuckled. "Yes, lots... and yes, *lots.*"

He smiled, although he didn't seem to be paying much attention to her words.

After what seemed like time had frozen again, Charlotte became aware of a hand on her arm and the sound of Maria's voice. "My dears... my dears? Antonio... our Charlotte here is now your great-grandmother's favourite. She has disliked most people for years, and now this wonderful girl has managed to charm her within a matter of minutes. Thank you so much. Juana fell right asleep, which is rare for her... you are so kind."

"I'm not surprised to hear this," said Antonio "Wonderful doesn't come close, Mama." He stared lovingly at Charlotte, who saw Maria looking between them out of the corner of her eye.

"Let's go outside, my dears. I want to show our guest the gardens. Come, Antonio. Do you have a drink, Charlotte?"

Charlotte absent-mindedly looked around and realised her drink had gone and remembered her hands were still oily.

"Ah. No, I think I'll need another one! I'm just going to pop to the loo and wash my hands. Please go on without me, I'll only be a jiff!"

Saying hello to a couple of people on the way, Charlotte found the entrance to that wing of the house and started down the hallway as per Maria's instructions. The faded carpet runner paired beautifully with the polished wooden floorboards, the stylish dusty-red walls and numerous framed pictures.

As Charlotte slowed down to look at one particular photo, a black and white picture of the front of the house, she felt someone aggressively squeeze her left arm and shove her against the wall. Catching the edge of a particularly large picture frame in the middle of her forehead, Charlotte saw stars as she was swung around roughly by her arm and pushed against the wall.

An angry, red face was centimetres from hers, and an elbow was pressing across her neck. Lucia looked crazed; her normally beautiful face monster-like with teeth bared. Having broken up several fights during her country upbringing, Charlotte was used to physical aggression but normally there was a warning. Fear now flickered in her core as Lucia spoke.

"Listen, you little *bitch*. This family is *mine*. Do you understand? Not yours, *mine*. I've done the time with these idiots, and I'm not giving it up to some stupid convict from the gutter. Understand?"

Flickers of spit hit Charlotte in the face. Head still swimming from the blow, her legs wobbled and gave a window of opportunity to free herself from Lucia's vice-like stance. She instinctively cupped her forehead as Lucia continued.

"Antonio is my *husband*, you slut! I've seen the way you look at him and follow him around. And my children! How you manipulate them, just so they'll like you... it's pathetic. Do you make a habit of going after happily married men? Ha! Good luck with your ugly face! You think you can steal him from me? Especially now that I'm carrying his third baby?" She rubbed her belly with a smug grin spreading across her face. Charlotte's eyes widened, and she placed both hands behind her on the wall, steadying herself.

"You're... pregnant?" Charlotte asked dopily, hardly believing her ears.

Lucia's grin widened, making her now look reptilian. "Yes, I am... and it's Antonio's. A boy." She came closer, grabbing Charlotte's arm and pinning her against the wall, her voice lowered to almost a whisper. "Why don't you just leave. No one wants you here. I'm providing Antonio with a son and an heir to the family name. What are you providing? A hand massaging service?"

Lucia stepped back again and turned as footsteps approached.

"Pardon me, is everything alright here?" asked Tim, the same waiter who assisted Charlotte earlier, with concern on his face. "Miss, are you alright?"

"She's fine, waiter," Lucia replied cheerfully. "Just a little too much champagne!"

"Very good," Charlotte heard him say, but detected some disbelief in his tone.

Charlotte was staring at Lucia's high-heeled feet, unable to move or think.

"Go clean yourself up, you look like shit! Worse than usual. If you tell anyone about this, your name will be mud in this town. Clear? Just go home, leave us alone. We don't need your sort around here—slut!"

Avoiding eye contact, Charlotte felt the force of her words. Her blurry vision made her feel nauseous. As Lucia walked away, Charlotte rushed through the empty bathroom and into a cubicle before vomiting into the basin. Her knees felt cold on the hard slate flooring, and her forehead was throbbing. Thankfully, she had hardly consumed any food in the afternoon due to her busy schedule, and the retching was comprised of mostly air. She flushed the toilet, stood up shakily and sat on the now closed lid. Feeling the tears come, Charlotte's previous elation plunged like the brick in her empty stomach.

She's pregnant. Lucia is pregnant, with Antonio's baby...

After some time, a resolution formed in Charlotte's head. Heart heavy and head pounding, she stood, came out of the cubicle and splashed cold water on her face at the sink. Looking up into the mirror, she saw a large welt on her forehead; the reddened mark matching her red-rimmed eyes. Lucia was right; she looked a mess. Wiping her eyes and patting her face dry, she leaned on the counter and took a deep breath. Her resolve now set, she knew what she needed to do.

Upon opening the bathroom door, she saw Maria, Antonio and Lucia standing together a little way up the hallway, turning to face her as she reappeared. Maria and Antonio rushed over.

"Oh my God, darling, are you alright?" Antonio asked, his hand going instinctively to Charlotte's forehead. "What happened?"

Maria's arm snaked around her back and Charlotte flinched instinctively as Lucia stepped forward to answer on her behalf.

"I found her in the hallway, holding her head," said Lucia. "Did you trip over or something? You're so clumsy, Charlotte."

Charlotte felt Maria's hand on her back and another touch her arm, protectively.

"What did you do, were you trying to walk in those heels?" Lucia added, sneering while rubbing her stomach.

Charlotte furrowed her brow but winced in pain. "I'm... I hit my head on the picture. I'm so sorry, guys. I'm going to have to go home. I'm... I'm not feeling well at all." She saw the concern on Antonio and Maria's faces.

Lucia smirked and stayed silent.

"Are you sure, my dearest girl? You are welcome to rest here, can we look after you?" Maria patted her arm gently.

Charlotte smiled weakly and shook her head. "Thank you, Maria, you're lovely. I would like to leave though please. I need to go home."

Tears pricked in Charlotte's eyes and the words felt heavier than she intended.

I need to go home.

Antonio seemed to sense something, and his face fell, searching Charlotte's face for an answer. She broke her gaze with him and looked down at the carpet.

"How fortunate you were passing by, Lucia," said Maria with an acidic tone as they ushered their guest towards the living room. "You certainly are a good Samaritan. I'm interested to see the video footage of how kind you were to our Charlotte when she had an *accidental* stumble."

Not wishing to engage in any more conflict, Charlotte kept her face lowered.

"Lucia, don't go anywhere," Antonio stated with an air of barely contained anger. "I have some questions for you." He took his phone out and held it up to his ear.

"I'll be right here waiting for you, my darling," said Lucia sweetly as the three departed, leaving her in the hallway.

"Yes, Hugo, could you please put Char's bicycle in the car. She needs to go home now. Yes... well she's had an accident but she's walking. I will check and let you know. Thanks."

Antonio replaced his phone in his pocket as they moved through the living room, with Charlotte attracting some concerned looks from the partygoers.

"Hugo would like to know if you wanted him to take you to the hospital?" Antonio asked.

Charlotte gave a small smile and shook her head.

"Let me grab your bag. Mama, will you be okay to take Char out the front?"

Maria responded immediately. "Of course, my dear." As they approached the front door, Maria asked, "Oh, Tim, can I please talk to you in a moment?"

"Yes, Ma'am. Does Miss Charlotte need anything?"

"We are alright, thank you, Tim. See, everyone here adores you, my dear,"

Charlotte felt more tears stream down her face; Lucia's cruel words were mixing discordantly with Maria's sweet ones. Her upbringing loomed over her initial feelings of being so at home in this place... and now she was desperate to leave and never come back. Feeling the slight chill of the twilight air as they passed through the front doors, Charlotte launched herself sideways at Maria and held her in a tight embrace, sobbing.

"Oh, my darling!" said Maria. "What is it? Are you in pain? Why are you crying?"

They held each other for some time. Charlotte eventually released her host and stepped back, wiping her tear-streaked face with the backs of her hands. She looked up at the beautiful house and then at Maria, sniffing uncontrollably. "I've just... I've never been... thank you. Maria, I'm sorry, but I have to leave. I have to go home. You're so nice. Your family is so nice and welcoming to such a country bumpkin like me... or as some would say: a '*criminal.*'" She broke off as her voice wavered.

Maria squeezed Charlotte's hand and looked at her with determination. "Don't you dare call yourself that! And don't you dare listen to a word that comes out of that... that little *bitch's* mouth, you hear me? My dear... did she do this to you? Did Lucia hurt you? Did she say something? You were fine when you went to the bathroom... please, tell me... tell me what you mean by 'going home'... you do mean back to your apartment here, right?"

Charlotte's vision swam and she hiccoughed when she looked down. Wondering how to respond, Charlotte turned to see Hugo hurrying up the steps towards the women, addressing Charlotte first as he charged towards her.

"Miss Grant, are you alright? You hit your head; can I please take you to the doctor?" He could barely contain his concern.

Charlotte smiled, feeling warmed by the kindness shown to her. "Thank you, Hugo. I'm pretty tough. I don't need a doctor. I just..." She turned to Maria and Antonio, who had just appeared with her backpack.

"Here, Charlotte. Would you like me to come with you? You might be concussed."

She shook her head again with tears still streaming down her cheeks as she addressed her hosts. "You are such lovely people. Thank you for your hospitality and looking after me. I've really loved this time... with a real family. Antonio, you are just..." Charlotte paused as the golf ball stuck in her throat, "... you are my sunshine, too."

Maria's hand went to her heart and tears welled in her eyes.

Antonio's face was etched in confusion.

Without saying anything further, Charlotte turned and gave a small smile to Hugo as he took her hand, helping her climb into the limousine.

She looked back at the house one more time; it would be the last she'd see of it or the Sanchez family ever again.

www.ingramcontent.com/pod-product-compliance
Lightning Source LLC
LaVergne TN
LVHW020347260326
834688LV00045B/1585